DEMONS IN MY BLOODSTREAM

STORIES

CANDACE NOLA

DEATH'S HEAD PRESS

PRAISE FOR CANDACE NOLA

"Candace Nola has appeared on the hardcore horror scene in a huge splash of blood, soaking readers with her diabolical prose. Her work is both demented and delicious."
–Kristopher Triana
Author of *GONE TO SEE THE RIVER MAN*

"Candace Nola flits between sub genres like a chameleon shifting color to match its surroundings, all while consistently injecting horror and a sense of real danger into every story. Her words cut into the heart of the reader, digging through the darkest places to free the hope within. Even when it's only an ember, Nola manages to make it shine with her unique style."
–Brennan LaFaro
Author of the *SLATTERY FALLS* trilogy

"There's no doubt about it... Candace Nola is a storyteller of the highest degree. Whether it be pulling at your heartstrings or chilling your bones to the marrow, she delivers the literary goods time and time again."
–Ronald Kelly
Author of *FEAR* and *THE ESSENTIAL SICK STUFF*

Published by Death's Head Press,
an imprint of Dead Sky Publishing, LLC
Miami Beach, Florida
www.deadskypublishing.com

Cover by Don Noble
Edited by Anna Kubik
Copyedited by Zoe Lemmon

To the usual suspects: the kitty, the puddin', and the sir.
For Mom.

For the Unicorn.

DEMONS IN MY BLOODSTREAM

Demons in my bloodstream
Thriving on my pain
Twisting
Turning
Agony remains
Fiends filter through my soul
Ripping
Tearing
Holes in tattered cellophane
Frenzied ghosts wreak havoc in my mind
Haunting
Hating
Memories left behind
Fear consumes the rest of me
Rotting
Decaying
A corpse out of time
Demons in my bloodstream
Thriving on my pain
Feeding
Devouring
Delighting in my shame
Poison in my cells
Multiply
Amplify
My loathing and disgust
Tears flow from saltwater eyes
Wounds of copper and rust
Demons in my bloodstream
Gazing back at me
Cavorting as I bleed

IT'S SO PRETTY

CHAPTER ONE

S tanley Thompson was born color blind. Having a form of tritanopia, Stanley grew up adapting quite well to his life, which played out for him like an old movie: muted and dull. He had been a quiet boy, preferring numbers to people, books to biking, novels to nature, science to romance. Stanley's parents were horribly dull people too, both just as uninteresting as the world Stanley lived in.

Their home was a modest bungalow, with a small front lawn and a cement stone path that led from the sidewalk to the front door. A single flowering tree stood in the northeast corner and a sturdy row of hedges ran the length of their yard, front to back, separating it from their neighbors. Those same hedges formed a brusque square of the backyard and marched straight back up the opposite side of the front yard, ending at the white picket fence that cordoned off the front of the yard.

A single row of flower beds outlined the front of the bungalow, situated perfectly beneath each front window. The front door was white, with a glass storm door, and a black iron knocker right in the middle, directly above the mail slot. The home itself was painted a light gray, trimmed in charcoal.

When his parents learned that young Stanley would never see color like they did, Doris set about re-designing their world to match his muted one. Their vibrant yellow bungalow was painted over in "dove gray while the darker "stormy gray" trim offered a bleaker outline to the home's angles and edges. The daffodils under the windows were replaced with soft white and pink pansies. The grand oak in the northeast corner was cut down and replaced with a flowering white snowball tree. The trim on the fence, the gate and front door were all black, midnight black. The inside layout was just as plain as the outside, muted colors and plain, practical furniture.

Doris marched through Stanley's young life searching for every shade of white, gray, black, and drab color in-between, so intent she was on Stanley being able to at least understand the slight differences between the few colors that he could see. But Stanley didn't see, nor did he much care.

He had more interesting things to explore. Like numbers! Now, those were black and white, no shades of gray there. Stanley could do complicated equations in his head before he was ten years old, not only adding and subtracting, but fractions and division, too.

His CPA father was pleased as punch to see his young son so studious and so quickly adapting to the job that he did so proudly. Thomas Thompson took great joy in teaching his son numbers, equations, and accounting. By the time young Stanley was twelve, he had a plastic visor cap to match his father's and a nifty pocket protector of his own.

There they sat, side by side, in their monochromatic home, fingers blazing across adding machines, doing up taxes and accounts for friends, neighbors, and business owners from town. Stanley took over the household budget at fourteen and took over his parents' stocks at sixteen. He kept them in the black, no red here, no red ever.

He was isolated, sheltered, and dull, but it was a life, and he lived it well. Whatever Stanley set his mind to, he excelled. He never bemoaned his lot in life. He never smeared dirt on their white walls, nor scuffed the black baseboards with his shoes. He never kicked despairingly at the pathetic pansies beneath the window.

He understood his mother's love better than she did. She lived in fear that he would one day be suddenly able to see all the colors and, just like that, realize that his home life was a lie. That his parents looked nothing like he thought they should. That his clothes, his things, his home would all become instantly alien to him and he would feel betrayed. Doris feared he would have a *Wizard of Oz* moment, his world suddenly going from muted tones to bright technicolor rainbows.

He felt sorry for her, even though he never told her not to worry. He just went on about his isolated existence. She loved color, craved its brightness. Not once during his childhood did she ever complain about their monochromatic home with their white walls and black trim. Sterile, functional, hopelessly bland, but she did it for Stanley.

She wanted him to see that a white wall was the color he saw, that the black dots on her dress and the blackbirds in the paintings on the wall were the same, that the gray dove was the color of a storm front on a rainy day, a gentle blending of Stanley's only color scheme. She tried awfully hard to keep only colors he could see around the house, but she couldn't give up her red lips.

She loved lipstick, deep crimson gloss over her full lips. To Stanley, it looked black. He never would have known; except he saw her secret bag of colors one day. The gray pouch of lipsticks and polish that all carried labels like "luscious berry," "divine wine," and "cherry pop." Labels that looked like all the others on the vanity but those said, "midnight black," "starry moon," and "heavy metal gray."

They all looked black, except Stanley finally knew they weren't. Puzzled, he sat in his room and thought, why hide the colors that he couldn't see? It all looked the same to him. He didn't mind, or wouldn't have, except now he did. She was sad, he realized. Sad that her life was like his, dull, like rainy days and wintertime.

She always told him things were fine, that one day he would see how pretty things could really be, how pretty colors were, how bright the world truly was.

"Just wait and see, my dear boy, one day you'll wake up, healed and new and it'll be so pretty!" As she pulled out her special tube of "divine wine" and glided it over her lips, smacking them and rubbing them together for a perfect pout, quietly muttering, "it's just so pretty," when she thought he couldn't hear.

She muttered the same phrase when she wore her gothic black and steel gray lipsticks, too. Mostly trying to convince herself, rather than Stanley. He didn't really care, he never had. If anything, he never understood why she thought the black gleaming stain on her mouth looked pretty, more like an open rotting wound, festering and decaying, rotting her lips from inside out. But now, being older, he understood why she suffered so. She gave up her bright colors for her unfortunate son, a sacrifice she never had to make.

CHAPTER TWO

By twenty-one, he had made his parents wealthy and sent them on their way. He bought their bungalow for himself, sent them abroad, and purchased a new modern condo on the beach, decorated in as much color as the designer was able. That was his way of saying thank you for being perfectly adequate parents.

Once that matter had been settled, he set up a lab in the basement for his research. In came books, beakers, and boxes. Here came scopes, slides, and sponges. Scopes, both big and small, desks, files, and research tools of all sorts. Stanley was determined to cure his color blindness. His only wish was to fulfill his mother's deepest dream of her son being able to experience the world as she did.

His existence had made hers miserable. He swore he would fix it one day and give the colors back. He'd already bought the beach house, full of light and color, but now he would complete the next step.

Join them in seeing color, wearing color, and learning color. He would find the prettiest colors just to show her that he understood what she gave up for him. Stanley would see all the colors and he would bring her the prettiest one he could find. She would be so happy. And together they would gaze upon it, and she would murmur in awe, "It's just so pretty," and Stanley, finally, would be able to agree.

CHAPTER THREE

Stanley had a plan, and he moved forward with it meticulously.

He had piles of research on fascinating gene therapy trials that had been conducted on adult squirrel monkeys. The researchers had chosen this species since all male squirrel monkeys are red-green color blind. Human male ratios were not as severe, being one in twelve, but Stanley was very close to the top of that scale.

The monkeys had been injected with a treatment designed to give them the missing L-opsin gene that they lacked. The researchers were confident the therapy would work, in theory. They didn't know if the brain would be able to process the new input, but regardless, Stanley was determined to try. He purchased the items to recreate the experiment on himself.

Weeks passed as Stanley spent every night and entire weekends locked in his lab, testing and retesting injection formulas, gene combinations, and synthetic drugs. Each one failing; each one pushing his obsession further.

Stanley added holistic changes to his diet. He started a strict regimen of vitamins and supplements known to increase eye health. Powders, capsules, shakes, and rubs, oils and ointments were all introduced to his routine. Lutein, Zinc, B1 and Omega-3, Bilberry, and Gingko, all joined the mix. He ate carrots, spinach, and fish with almost every meal. He was already fit and healthy and exercised daily, but the stricter diet was adding to his muscle mass as an added bonus. Stanley Thompson, once scrawny and weak, was growing rapidly into a lean, strong, well-muscled young man.

Ninety days into his research, while taking a rare but much needed break to shower before a supply run, he looked in the mirror, startled at his appearance.

"What the hell?" he muttered to his reflection, eyes roving over his broadened chest and firmer biceps. For the first time, he had the beginnings of a six-pack. His face, while gaunt and sickly from lack of rest and sunshine, sat on the body of a new health nut. He chuckled as he turned to the side and flexed like a bodybuilder he had seen on television, grimacing in the mirror.

"I guess I'm doing something right." He splashed cold water on his face, trying to reduce the bags under his eyes. He strode naked to the bedroom, his chest puffed out just a bit more than it had been before, his walk a bit more powerful than it had been yesterday.

It was a bright day outside. His vision displayed the same muted landscape, but the soft shades he could see were even lighter than normal. He slid into his coupe and headed into town to grab groceries, supplies from the hardware store, and an order from the drugstore for his tests. He set off faster than his normal speed of thirty-five miles an hour in his residential area. Today, Stanley Thompson was testing limits. Today, he pressed the gas to forty-five as he left the cul-de-sac.

He finished the first couple of stops quickly, then headed for the organic market. Stanley ate the freshest foods he could find, and his income allowed him to afford the best. Imported seafood went into his cart, followed by choice cuts of meat, ostrich, veal, and buffalo, the best vegetables, and a whole host of fruit. He was disciplined and obsessed with his dietary needs to ensure the best response for his experiments. When Stanley Thompson committed to something, he *fully* committed.

When a shapely young woman approached him with a friendly smile, he raised one eyebrow quizzically, surprised.

"Hi," she said, "I think this fell out of your cart." She held out a small bottle of Himalayan salt to him.

He looked at her, then down at the jar, not quite sure of what to say. Finally, he took it from her, feeling his skin beginning to grow warm under his collar.

"Umm... thanks. I guess I didn't notice," He mumbled awkwardly, not sure of what to do next. He put the bottle in his cart and stuck out his hand. "I'm Stanley Thompson."

"I'm Cara," she said, shaking his hand. "Cara Bronson. It's nice to meet you, Stanley." She smiled again, her eyes lingering on him a moment too long. His hand was still clinging to hers.

Quickly, he pulled his hand back, wiping the sweaty palm on his trousers as he did so. "Well, umm, thanks again for the salt. I'll just be on my way." Stanley gripped the handle of his cart and rushed towards the cash registers up front.

As Stanley piled groceries into his car, he berated himself for his stupid behavior with the woman. He had never had a girlfriend, rarely interacted with them, choosing his books and numbers instead. He knew women were impressed by colors, by fashion, art, and flowers. All the things his mother loved but had never taught him.

Stanley could not even tell if the woman had truly been blond or brunette. She had shoulder-length hair of a light color, wore slender jeans that stopped just above her ankle, and a simple T-shirt that hugged her curves. Her smile had been radiant.

He thought about that smile as he left the parking lot at forty-five miles an hour.

After years of isolation, Stanley was thinking that having a female companion in his life might be possible. He felt his heartbeat pick up as former idle thoughts suddenly presented themselves as possibilities.

Stanley was experiencing actual arousal and excitement for the first time since puberty, and his pulse thrummed in his ears. His heart beat against the cage of his chest a little harder. He entered the cul-de-sac at a feisty fifty miles an hour, kicking gravel up as he made the turn. His smile was just a little wider.

CHAPTER FOUR

Back inside his small house, Stanley's focus returned to full force. All thoughts of the woman were sent to the back of his mind as he set about his evening routine, but she lingered there all the same, in flashes of bright smiles and white teeth.

He prepared a meal of grilled fish and vegetables, then tossed a large serving of greens, carrots, vitamins, and supplements into his juicer, and drank that. Stanley found himself smiling several times as flashes of Cara entered his mind unbidden, but not unwelcome. When the food was done, he ate, then took a bottle of water to the lab, ready to work until the wee hours of the morning.

Stanley prepared test slides for his bloodwork and made another mixture for the gene therapy injection. He pushed the button on the computer to record, and then the first injection of concentrated vitamins and drugs went into his veins. He waited patiently, gritting his teeth, as the fluid burned a trail through his system.

He documented the test number of the concentrated serum so he could reference it if he had positive results. He took careful notes of his physical reactions: temperature, pulse, trembling, blurry vision or floaters in his eyes, sweating, or nausea. Anything that could prove useful later. There was no evidence that one could even get results, but the research on the monkeys had worked. He figured that higher doses of the same ingredients would work on a human. That was just logical thinking.

He was determined to find a way to see color, any color, something he could share with his mother. He wanted desperately to understand the one thing she loved most: deep reds and majestic blues, royal purples. He remembered she had tried to explain it to him as she read him picture books. Her face became animated when she tried to impress the colors upon him in words, but none of those words could ever define "color" for him. He saw her sad expression and the twinkle in her eyes dim over time as she resorted to saying things like "it's a lighter gray" or "this one looks almost black."

Pastel yellows, pinks, and greens often appeared muted beige or tans, while most others appeared as blends of gray, muted brownish-green and black. A constant pea soup consistency of a life. He wanted to understand the delight in her eyes when she glided the bright red lipstick over her lips, thinking he couldn't tell the difference. The tubes had different names for red. He could pick up the slight difference in the black sheen of the "crimson apple" when she wore it, and the matte black of the "metal gray" tube she kept in her purse.

He hated that she felt like she had to live the same muted life as him. Though he knew she did it out of her love for him; her desire that he not feel alone had isolated him so much more than she had ever realized. Rather than help him adjust to the world around him, she had tried to force their world to adjust to him.

Instead of giving him learning aids and tools to get him through public school, she had homeschooled him, using workbooks and online classrooms. Instead of taking him out to learn the bus systems, subways, and sports games, she had kept him at home, where things were easy to control.

Interactions with other kids were rare. He hardly went out, never had a friend or a lover, and never worked outside of his home. Her efforts to pretend as if things were normal had damaged his perspective of the world and the people in it. Stanley grew up thinking that people would not accept him, that they would somehow be able to tell that he was diminished or lesser than them because he only saw the barest shades of the world around them. The lady at the store today did not seem to notice anything was amiss. Stanley wondered if he had been wrong all along, if he could be a part of the world, despite his view of it.

Stanley shrugged and shook off the idle thoughts. He had made a vow for his mother, and he intended to keep it. Stanley kept his word. His father taught him that a man was only as good as his word. His mother deserved his best. He finished his notes, then set them aside. He needed to prepare new test slides while the drug was fresh in his veins.

His head throbbing, he rose and stepped around the table. His vision was growing spotty and dim. Stanley shook his head and blinked rapidly, trying to see through the sudden fog. He continued walking, then suddenly, darkness hit him, and he fell face-first into the glass shelves of his lab.

He came to in seconds, groaning in pain. He lay face down in a cabinet, shards of glass poking into his flesh every time he moved. A strange foggy cloud filled his mind and his sight; shiny, dark fluid coated every surface he saw. Blood gleamed under the light like his mother's crimson lipstick.

He stood, woozy, biting back a scream. His reflection in the remaining glass pane showed blood running from cuts on his face, his neck, arms, and hands. Pieces of glass stuck out of him, piercing through his trousers and shirt, slicing him open.

Cursing and fascinated, he looked at the floor, at the blood pooled there, then at the cabinets where thin rivers of it ran. He ran his hands along his face and smeared the wetness across his cheeks. A hint of something appeared in his vision, a murky aura, not gray, black, or white. Something new, shiny, and bright, something that he had no notion of but knew was right.

RED.

It was red that he saw, right at the edge of his vision. Red gleamed and lingered and faded like stars. He knew blood was red. His mother had said it was. He remembered cutting his finger once on a staple while helping his father. It had hurt and felt wet, not cold but warm like his bathwater. He had gone to her crying, and she bandaged it up, soothing and teaching him in her melodic voice.

He stood staring, blinking the blood from his eyes, smiling as red filled his vision. He plucked out more glass, gasping in pain, as the red brightened, then faded. He plucked once again, deep red flashed in front of his eyes, twice more, he pulled glass from his neck and face. Again, the red cloud filled the edges of his vision, surrounded by black, gray, and white.

He pushed on each piece gently, relishing the crimson glow that swam before him, then twisting it until he screamed, rewarded with a clear display of crimson on black and white. This was art. This was beauty. He finally understood what his mother missed most, the sheer joy of a colorful world. He wept tears of pain and joy as he tried to make the color last, but each time he removed a piece, the color faded from sight.

His vision cleared and focused; his lab came into stark view, bright white floors, tables, and cabinets, black microscopes, ink pens, and chairs. Bright scarlet streamed from his face, the walls, and doors where he fell. RED. He saw it fully, clearly, then he blinked, and it was gone, faded to gleaming, glistening black. Stanley Thompson began to grin, standing in his lab, bloody and panting in pain, his smile stretched wide. He could *see* it.

When he started to sway on his feet, he moved from the lab into the bathroom to finish removing the glass. He stripped and washed his wounds clean, standing naked on the tile. Blood streamed down his body, making sticky crimson footprints around him as he struggled to bandage the punctures and cuts. Pain broke through his euphoria as he staggered through the house to collapse on his bed.

CHAPTER FIVE

When Stanley woke the next day, sunlight poured through the slats of his blinds. Searing pain rippled through his body as he stumbled to the bathroom. His vision flared with glimmering red as the pain intensified. Stanley clutched at the wall, the door frame, and the marble sink as he made his way to the shower. His head pounded, and his ears filled with static. He flipped the shower on, then turned and vomited into the toilet, retching and heaving as stomach acid filled the bowl.

Taking deep breaths, he swayed woozily over the toilet and

talked himself through breathing until the dizziness passed. When he was able to stand steadily, the sound of running water came back to him and he gingerly limped over to the steaming shower.

His body was a mass of punctures, scabs, and ragged tears, each one tender to touch and showing a brown-black coloring around the edges. Stanley knew now that it was red, not black. It was the crust of blood covering the scabs, peeking around the edges, and caked on his skin. Blood coated most of the wounds and he watched as the water coursed down his body, rinsing the blood from his skin. It tinged the water as it swirled around his feet, turning murky as it fled down the drain.

He finished his shower, groaning as he stepped over the edge of the tub. If he could fully see his body as others did, he would see how his skin glowed bright red from the heat of the water, and the dozens of marks on his skin were flushed pink, red, and purpled with bruises. His sandy brown hair stuck up all over his head, tears ran from the jagged cut that began in the corner of his left eye and down his cheek. The wounds ran jagged lines across his face, neck, chest, and down both arms. A long gash ran along his thigh. Bloody handprints from the night before marred the sink and floor, drops led into the hallway, and all the way back to the lab.

"That'll leave a nice scar," he muttered, peering at his face in the mirror. The injuries appeared as various shades of muted brown, yellow, and black. He sighed. He was not cured.

A thought occurred to him then, and curious, he stuck a finger into the deepest gash on his thigh, gasping at the pain. The gasp turned into a guttural groan as he twisted deeper into the cut, tearing the gash open wide. The red aura bloomed as he jabbed deeper into his flesh. RED. Bright, deep color ripped into his vision. It blossomed at the edges of his eyesight, then came into focus as blood dripped down his leg. Fresh and sparkling and just so pretty.

He pulled his finger out, only part of the way, holding the flesh apart as he inspected it. Red tissue glistened prettily as he bit his own tongue to prolong the pain. Red was all he saw. His heart expanded, then exploded with joy as he saw the crimson, the scarlet, all the reds in between on his hands, on his skin, on the floor. Glorious red. He smiled, sobs choking him.

"It's just so pretty," he said to himself, "so pretty." He reached out to the mirror, trailing bloody fingers down the glass. The echo of his mother's voice played in his mind, and he smiled widely, saying the phrase again.

When the color vanished from his vision, anger flared deep inside him. He reared back and punched the mirror, shattering it as he cursed and raged. He pummeled the door and the wall outside his room. Screaming obscenities as he destroyed his bedroom. He took out his rage on his belongings, blood dripping across the floor and carpets from the still open gash in his leg. He hurled a lamp at the opposite wall, then collapsed to the floor, out cold from blood loss and pain.

CHAPTER SIX

Stanley woke to the ruins of his room in the early evening light. He found his lamp miraculously still in one piece, turned on the light, and inspected the seeping wound on his leg. It was deep, deeper than he expected, and too wide for him to close with a bandage. Most importantly, the red was gone. He sighed, defeated, staring at the rusty brown smears oozing from the gash on his leg.

Whatever breakthrough he thought he had made, it was gone. His leg would need stitches before he could continue with his work. He thought of his lab and the mess that was waiting for him. He groaned, stood up, and got dressed. His wallet was in the mess on the floor. He grabbed it and, slipping his feet into a pair of sneakers, he headed to his car.

The hospital was brightly lit and hurt his eyes, but the nurse was kind and efficient. She saw the state of him and took him to an exam room. It took her twenty minutes to clean his wounds and bandage the minor ones. The doctor was needed for the rest. The doctor entered ten minutes later, followed by the nurse, who began preparing a tray of tools and bandages. He greeted him politely as he began to do a quick exam.

"My nurse tells me that you passed out and fell into a glass cabinet. Is that right?" the doctor asked, gaining the details he needed.

"Yes. I was finishing my work and went to put away some supplies. I hadn't eaten much and guess I passed out." Stanley shrugged, feigning a sheepish expression that didn't quite look believable. It was more like a cross between constipation and anger.

"Tough break. Carpeted floors, hardwood?" the doctor asked, flashing a light in each eye.

"Tile floors in my office," Stanley replied, blinking from the sudden burst of white light.

"Headaches before this? Any nausea or new medicine?" The doctor sat on the stool and began preparing Stanley's leg for the stitches, wiping the surrounding area heavily with iodine wipes and sterile gauze.

"No, nothing new. A few vitamins," Stanley said, watching the liquid on his leg run down the sides, deep black mixed with a lighter color, which he knew to be the iodine the doctor had used. His chest tightened with anger.

"Alright, well, I don't see any signs of a concussion but come in if you start experiencing things like severe headaches, memory loss, sudden dizziness, double vision, be sure to come back in." The doctor spoke as he prepared to stitch Stanley's leg.

"This might sting at first. It'll numb quickly," he said.

Stanley gasped as the red aura flared at the edges of his vision, then was gone as the numbing agent began to work.

"Are you okay?" The doctor looked up, concern on his face.

"Yes, fine," Stanley replied.

When he got home, he would clean the lab and then recreate the serum he had used the night before. He would use a stronger injection too, more concentrated. The wheels in his brain were already turning. He would bring the red back: the red, the scarlet, the crimson, the purples, the pinks. He would bring all the colors back now that he knew he could, but above all else, Stanley would bring back the red.

"You are all set, Mr. Thompson. The nurse will be back shortly with your discharge papers, and you will be free to go. Just come back if you experience any signs of infection or a concussion. Warning signs will be fully described in the paperwork."

"Thanks, I will," Stanley shook his hand and nodded politely as the doctor left the room.

A few minutes later, discharge papers in hand, Stanley limped from the double doors of the hospital, a new plan already in mind, pain forgotten.

CHAPTER SEVEN

Back home, he began the tedious job of cleaning his room and his lab. He scrubbed the blood away, swept the glass shards from the floor, and ordered a new pane of glass for his cabinet. He placed another order for scalpels, razor blades, and other tools. Finally, he sat down and began formulating the blend for the serum.

There were flashes of red, multiple times; that had been real, and he had been able to make it happen again. His vision had to be restoring itself somehow. He just needed to ramp up his efforts. Smiling to himself, he jotted down more notes and pulled up his research on the computer.

Getting cut had somehow triggered the flashes of red, but was it the pain or the adrenaline that caused it? Was it a mental trigger or a physical one, and how could he prove either one? He understood that he could not keep cutting himself to see it again. He needed the color in his life now; he needed to see the dark scarlet stain spread across his skin, his walls, his life.

He understood now why his mother had yearned for it. Surely, it was the most beautiful of all the colors. The color of life, of the hearts, of the inner human construct, the sole color used for love. He no longer cared about any other color but red.

"It's so pretty," he whispered to himself as he pictured it in his mind.

When he learned how to see it fully, all the time, then he could share his joy with his mother. She would be so pleased. Maybe even Cara, the woman from the store, he could share it with her too. She must shop at that store often. He would just go, and he would see her. Yes, he would see her again and share the red with her, too.

He checked his machines, slid the test slides into the cooler, and headed to his room for the night. His brain was firing on all pistons, already ten steps ahead. Stanley Thompson had a new drug, and he was already addicted. Red memories pulsed in his brain, flashing like a bar sign on a stormy night. Neon bright, humming like an electrical current in his pulse.

CHAPTER EIGHT

The next few weeks passed in a blur as he continued his experiments with his gene therapy and made frequent trips to the market, lingering in the aisles and in his car, hoping to see Cara. He finally caught a glimpse of her entering the store on a sunny afternoon, just as he was about to pull out of the parking lot.

Quickly, he pulled into a parking space once again. Inside, he grabbed a small basket and began casually scanning the aisles for her. She was near the dairy aisle. His heartbeat quickened as he approached her.

Stanley glanced around, suddenly unsure of what to say, but grateful that no one was nearby to see his clumsiness. Something flared in his brain, his body in the mirror a few weeks ago, the broad shoulders, the thicker biceps, his abs beginning to show definition. He smiled, puffing his chest out with more confidence.

He strode over to where she stood, casually reaching beside her to snag a package of yogurt from the shelf. He pretended to study it, put it back, then picked up another one, glancing up at her as he did so.

"Oh hey, Cara, right?" He said, "I didn't see you there."

"Hi" she replied, her smile widening in recognition. "Stanley, right? Oh my, what happened?" Cara asked as she studied his face, seeing the fresh pink scars and scratches that were not fully healed.

"Oh, umm. Small accident at home. I'm fine," He said with a shrug. "How are you?" Stanley asked, feeling his neck begin to flush with heat. His heart pounded as he stared a little too long at her smile. It made her eyes twinkle. He felt his own smile stretch. His cheeks hurt as the wounds pulled taut from the effort.

"Looks like it was more than small. I'm glad you're okay, though. I'm great. You know, the usual weekend errands." She laughed, and it was music to his ears.

"Yes. I am doing the same. I realized I had forgotten a few things and had to come back inside."

"Lucky for me then, huh?" She smiled at him and added several cups of yogurt and cottage cheese to her cart.

"I suppose we better get what we need," He said, stammering over the delivery a little as he tried to figure out what else to say.

"I guess so. Maybe I'll see you around again. Be more careful at home, okay?" Her eyes lingered on him, her smile shining with radiance. He caught the scent of her, fresh peaches, luscious and ripe. He thought she smelled like summer. No, that wasn't quite right. He smiled as it came to him. She smelled like sunshine.

Stanley watched her, yogurt cups forgotten, his smile fading as she disappeared down the next aisle. He bolstered himself once more as a flash of RED entered his mind. He could do this. She would understand RED, the beauty of it, how it made him feel. Of course she would. He could tell from her smile that she would understand. She was beautiful, so she would *know* beautiful. It was simple.

He straightened up once more, pulled his shoulders back, and hurried toward the aisle Cara had taken.

"Um, hey Cara?" He said as he approached, not wanting to startle her.

She turned around, smiling broadly. "Yes?"

"I don't really do this, but would you want to maybe get a coffee or have lunch sometime?" he asked, his eyes pulled to her smile once more. It felt warm, like standing in the sun.

"Sure, I'd like that he answered. "Do you have a cell phone on you?" she asked, holding her hand out.

"Yea, right here." He pulled it from his pocket and gave it to her, unlocking it with his thumb. She entered her phone number and called herself. She added her info to the contact card and handed it back. Then she saved his phone number on her phone.

"There you go. Call me or text me. I have plans this afternoon, but if you want to call me tomorrow, we can figure it out then, okay?" She beamed at him; another direct ray of sunlight heated his body from within.

"Great, thanks! I'll do that. I'll see you soon," she said as she turned back to her cart with a small wave.

He stood staring after her, white noise pounding in ears, with his heart racing. She had said yes. Stanley Thompson had asked a woman out for the first time. His breath caught in his throat and snakes squirmed in his gut. Stanley got in his car, a grin on his face, and a little more swagger in his step and peeled out of the parking lot, taking off down the road at a cool sixty miles an hour.

CHAPTER NINE

The next day, he sent Cara a text message, having Googled what was customary these days for relationships. Per all the advice online, texting was currently the big trend. Casual, trendy, cool, he liked it. After she replied with a date and time for the next weekend for lunch, Stanley got back on Google, this time searching for lunch spots and conversation starters.

His search devolved from advice on dating to advice on sex,

which led to some of the most depraved porn sites he had ever stumbled across. Sure, he had seen porn before, but found it uninteresting. The images on his screen now could not be what women really wanted. No one could really want these things done to them. *Could they?*

From there, he moved on deeper into the chat forums, looking for others like him, those who couldn't see color. He needed to find a way to speed up his research. He was growing impatient. In his mind, the bright flashes of color dripping down his counters and walls, streaming from his legs and arms, smeared across his bed sheets and floor, were fading.

He found posts on ocular migraines and followed that thread. It sounded like what had happened to him when he had passed out the first time in the lab. He bookmarked it. He stumbled across posts that claimed they would see color when they were hurt or, interestingly enough, hurting someone else. By accident, of course, but they claimed to see red when this happened. Red flashed in his mind, spiraling along his synapses as the word brought forth the mental color burst.

He made another note. Kept searching. One thread led to another, that led to another. It was midnight before he even noticed he had yet to prepare his injection of supplements and ill-gotten prescription drugs.

When he finished, he sat back down and pulled his notebook out to take notes. Something in the online discussions kept pulling at a connection in his brain.

Seeing red. Turning red. Flushed with anger. I was so angry I saw red. It hurt so much that I saw red.

So many comments about seeing red linked to pain and anger. Exactly like his accident and the next day, when he had prodded the gash in his leg until he passed out. The pain allowed him to see the color for what it was. Stanley couldn't recall having ever been so angry. Not until the day he destroyed his bedroom when the color went away. *Had he seen red that day?*

He injected the concentrated serum into his system, this time enhanced with steroids and testosterone. He shuddered as the potent fluid flooded his veins, burning like magma through his body. He gritted his teeth and slammed his hand down on the table, willing himself to sit and wait. His neck and jaw clenched as he struggled to withstand the pain.

He sat still, breathing slowly, focusing on the pain, embracing it, relishing the red flash when it finally bloomed behind his eyes. Stanley stood on shaky legs and walked to the supply cabinet. He removed a scalpel and slashed his arm open. The wetness blossomed in the razor-thin gash, then ran in a thin stream down his arm to his wrist and dripped from his pale fingertips. He stared at it, smiling as his vision clouded and then cleared. Another slash of the scalpel, more red appeared on pale flesh, seeping from the fresh wound and dripping to the floor.

Red. Red. Red. Crimson droplets on white tile. Drip. Drip. Drip.

It pulsed out in tune with his heartbeat. When the red began to fade, he made another cut, then another. It wasn't enough. It was fading too fast. His heart was racing as the color faded again. He needed something more.

Adrenaline. Pain. Adrenaline. Pain. His heart pounded. His temples throbbed. White noise created static in his brain. Red. Pain. Red. Pain. Stanley Thompson headed for his car.

CHAPTER TEN

Stanley tore down the lane at ninety miles an hour, seeking out a new experiment. His hands shook as drugs swam through his system and he headed downtown. Stanley's temperature rose as he tore around another bend, kicking up gravel and dirt. The car sped into a tunnel like a bullet. The landscape blurred past him. His smile stretched across his face as the red bloomed, blocking his vision, but fading in and out with every beat of his heart.

RED. RED. RED. RED.

His foot pushed the pedal closer to the floor. His hands gripped the wheel, knuckles tight. His eyes darkened, his grin widened.

RED. RED. RED. RED.

It flashed in his brain. Seeing it was the only thing that mattered. His mother would be so proud when he showed her.

"It's so pretty...so pretty," He sobbed, gripping the steering wheel as the car screeched around a sharp curve.

There was a deafening crunching sound as Stanley's body snapped forward into the steering wheel, then bounced back the airbag deployed. Metal skimmed across metal as his car spun around at the mouth of the tunnel. A horrendous ringing filled his ears.

His car skidded into a culvert head on. He could only see the red. It consumed him, his vision, his brain, his very essence. He could feel it. He felt red. Bright, hot, red rage seethed in his veins. Stanley sat stunned in the car. Lights were flashing, but he was not sure if it was in his head or out.

He pushed on his car door, but it jammed. He tried again, throwing his weight against it. It refused to budge. Anger flared bright, rage burned along his veins. Cursing, he pulled his legs from the driver's seat well and moved into the passenger seat, where the door hung open, twisted on its hinges.

He stumbled out of the ruins of the metal shell and strode across the road. He felt no pain, nothing but red rage pulsing from his core. A second car lay on its side by the tunnel entrance, one door half-open, a body on the ground beside it, a second trying to crawl from the back window. Lights flashed from the wreckage, dying ruined taillights and brake lights and blinkers, switching on and off, mimicking Stanley's heated brain.

RED. RED. RED. RED.

He could hear the clicking, louder than the moans of pain coming from the mangled car before him. Stanley reached down and gripped the hand stretched out for help.

"Please, help me." A soft feminine voice pleaded.

Stanley pulled. He yanked the person upright, then slammed his fist into the face that he could barely see. His knuckles made contact with soft skin and the bones beneath shattered under his fist. He grinned as red fluid flew from the broken nose. It gushed over their face in a torrent. He reared back and slammed his fist into the weeping jaw, shattering the teeth as the person collapsed to the street.

He looked around him, seeing only red. Red car, red lights, the dark abyss of the tunnel that led into town. Then he saw the pale body of the driver on the ground. Red shirt and pale pants, glistening, shiny red everywhere he looked. He lifted his foot and stomped on their back, screaming incoherently as he voiced his rage to the night. Bones broke and shattered, the rib cage collapsed, and blood spurted from their mouth.

He heard whimpering behind him and turned back. The driver, a woman, was on her hands and knees, trying to crawl away. Stanley caught her. Yanking her back by her ankles, he flipped her over and wrapped his hands around her throat, snarling at her.

"Do you see it?" Stanley growled. "Do you see it?"

"Look at it!" he forced her head up higher, making her look at him. "Look how pretty!"

Her ruined mouth was a mass of jagged teeth and bone, lower jaw hanging at an odd angle as he shook her. Something itched at the back of his mind, apricots or peaches wafted through the air. He shook her again.

She gasped for air, blood spilling over her lips as she sucked in teeth fragments trying to breathe.

"St..Stan..ley?" she rasped out, voice ragged, as she peered at him from her one good eye.

Stanley blinked and shook his head. RED rage consumed him, heated him from within, was the only thing he could see. A ghost of sunshine lingered, something warm and bright behind the blood seething in his veins, but it wasn't important.

"Stan...ley...wh..at...what hap-pened?" she stuttered, groaning as she hung limply in his grip.

Stanley slammed her head into the pavement. Deep red spurted out from her fractured skull as he pounded her face harder into the asphalt. Stanley was grinning maniacally as the color splattered everywhere, his face was covered in it. The body in his hands was drenched in it. The cold road beneath him was swimming in it. Glorious, magnificent red.

He stood and dragged the body over to the pale car it had crawled out of, lifting it like a sack of potatoes, he began smearing the pulpy remains of the skull over the side panels, painting it red under the moonlight with the blood of Cara Bronson.

He coated every inch of the car that he could reach. When he saw nothing left but glistening RED under the amber streetlight, Stanley dropped the body to admire his work.

"It's so pretty," he whispered, touching his fingertips to the dripping car. "So very pretty."

He wept as he looked around him. Chaos and ruin, painted red. He turned and began to stagger down the dark street toward home.

CHAPTER ELEVEN

The next morning, soon after the sun rose high in the sky, a SWAT team broke into the cozy black and white bungalow where Stanley Thompson was raised.

Guns drawn; they stared in horror at the naked man they found crouching by the wall in the far corner of the living room. He had skinned himself alive, peeling the flesh from his body, then painting the walls with his blood, strip by bloody strip. Mounds of flesh lay scattered on the white tiles.

Stanley looked over, his skull poking through the ruined flesh of his face. A rictus grin lit him up from within, impossibly wide, broke through the pain he must have been in as he pointed to the walls.

"It's so pretty.... It's just so pretty!" he screamed as they carted him away.

"IT'S SO PRETTY!"

ROXIE'S LIST

CHAPTER ONE: DEATH OF A SAINT

Roxanne Lee Marshall was dead.

Joe Marshall sat with his head in his hands on his side of the bed they had shared for thirty years, contemplating this fact. His wild, sassy, bleached blonde, Roxie, gone and soon to be buried, would never call him a "right cheeky old bastard" again before flashing him that crooked grin he loved so much, the one that made her eyes twinkle. No more making her tea and toast in the morning. No more weekly grocery trips to the Organic Market or Trader Pete's. She loved Traders Pete's.

"Such good quality, such a great store." He could almost hear her voice now, her nasally Jersey girl accent slipping out again, though they lived in the Bronx now.

He sighed a deep, bone-rattling sigh, the kind of sigh that you can only utter when facing the burden that Joe faced today. He ran a calloused hand through his graying hair and stood up, knees popping, and reached for the blue suit jacket hanging neatly on the closet door.

∿

JOE SAT QUIETLY IN THE FRONT ROW OF WHITMAN'S FUNERAL HOME, GAZING silently at the woman who lay so peacefully in her blush pink casket, surrounded by cream blankets and cushions. She looked like an angel if angels came from the Jersey shore.

She had truly been a saint, so kind and generous to everyone, fiercely protective of her family and her friends. Roxie was tenacious and stubborn to the bone but more loyal than any woman on Earth. Roxie spent hours visiting the elderly shut-ins from the church, volunteering at the soup kitchen, and reading gospel stories to the little ones in the Sunday bible classes. She was beloved by many. Her bright smile lit up many rooms, and now it was gone.

Joe wondered how the make-up artist had captured her signature teased updo so perfectly, and the porno blue eye shadow was the exact shade that Roxie adored. Her generous cleavage was tucked tastefully into her favorite dress, a leopard print bodice with a sleek black skirt, split to her thigh, with a wide spandex belt that hugged her trim waistline. Joe knew if he peeked under the satin blanket, he would find black stiletto pumps on her dainty feet.

The funeral home was silent as Joe stared at her from his seat, a weird expression on his face. The funeral director would later describe it as grief almost swallowed by sheer bewilderment. Joe was staring at his wife as if he didn't fully know who she was, but was trying to commit every detail to memory.

The funeral director discreetly cleared his throat and stepped from the shadowed niche.

"Joe, it's time." He spoke gently to the grieving man, solemnly placing a hand on his shoulder.

Joe nodded, stood, and lurched towards the casket, almost knocking the apricot roses from the lid. The director steadied both him and the spray of roses, before stepping back several feet for Joe's last moments with his wife. There were no sobs, just a quiet sniff, a gentle touch of his hand to her rouged cheek before he reached down to straighten the crystal rosary in her hand. He turned, stepped to the head of the casket, and nodded at the director. He was ready.

The director slid the doors apart. The Marshall's family, friends, and neighbors began to flow into the room in a somber line, down the right side to sign the guest book, gaze at the many plants and flowers on display, before respectfully filing past Mrs. Roxanne Marshall in all her angelic glory before stopping briefly in front of Joe for a hug or a hearty handshake and a few words. Back up the left side, they went before filtering into the rows of wooden seats and murmuring amongst themselves.

"She looks beautiful," said their neighbor, Delores. "Can you believe it?" sniffed Gwen, Roxie's yoga partner. Her friend Angie patted her hand and shook her head. They would need a third for yoga.

"So tragic, poor Joe, ain't got no kids. He's all alone now," whispered Aunt Minnie, Joe's only remaining relative on his father's side. Her husband and daughter quietly shushed her, as her whisper was no longer quiet, at least, not like the 90-year-old woman thought it was.

And so it went. Murmurs, whispers, and tear-filled sniffles filled the room, then ceased when the funeral director led Joe to his seat. On either side of Joe were his best buds, Vinnie and Vito. Large Italian men in black suits, with slicked-back hair, shiny shoes, and gold rings. They looked like mobsters flanking their unassuming accountant. They were the epitome of mafia men from the old classic movies, and they knew it, idealized it in their youth, and portrayed it now as men. Others respected them, perceived their tough guy routine for the power it was, and for the power that stood behind them. They were an odd trio, always had been, and they liked it that way. Joe sat stiffly, staring ahead. So, it began.

Afterward, a small luncheon was held at Maria's. A lovely place owned by Vinnie and Vito's sister. The banquet room had been reserved and Joe sat at the center table, smiling soberly at the line of mourners. His blue eyes were piercing and a bit too wide behind his wireframes. His blue suit hung limply from his slender frame, but Roxie always loved him in blue. *"Wear the blue one, Joe."* He could hear her voice now. *"You look so dapper in the blue."* It's not like he had time to buy a new one; Roxie's death had been so unexpected. The heart attack killed her instantly last Sunday morning as she prepared their breakfast. *"So handsome in the blue, Joe, just so handsome."* Her voice echoed in his thoughts.

Shadows clung beneath his eyes. It wasn't just the fact that Roxie had died. It was what he had found after that had him reeling internally while he tried to appear calm and stoic on the outside. He gave a sudden start as Vito clapped him on the back, asking if he was alright. Joe blinked rapidly, looking up at his friend, declining his offer of more food or drink.

Thankfully, Vinnie began shooing people away, asking them to let Joe finish his meal. Grateful for the sudden reprieve, Joe sat back in his chair and retreated within himself once more. The low murmur of voices remained a constant insectoid buzzing in his ears.

Roxie. Roxie. Roxie. What a surprise, indeed. Joe sat, mulling over his marriage and the discovery he had made. He thought he knew her; knew everything she knew: her hopes, her dreams, and her darkness. He knew about her abortions, about her abusive uncle, and the cousin that had drowned. He knew about the affair she once had before she had met Joe, with a married older man. He thought he knew all her secrets, but Joe had clearly been mistaken.

CHAPTER TWO: SECRETS

Joe sat at the old Formica kitchen table, nursing a Pabst blue ribbon, staring down at a faded notebook. The late afternoon sun streamed in through the kitchen window, broken into bright slivers by the backyard fencing.

The day had been long and draining and Joe's anxiety had almost gone through the roof before Vinnie and Vito had taken him home. His left eye had begun to twitch, the longer he sat in the stuffy banquet hall overrun with funeral flowers and old lady perfume.

Now he was staring at the object of his despair. A simple blue notebook faded but filled with Roxie's handwriting. Not quite a journal, more of a book of simple thoughts, musings, observations, and a rather peculiar list.

It was the list that bothered him. The rest made him sad, simple thoughts that Roxie had over the years. The silent observation of her life. Joe had tried very hard to be a good husband, and evidence of that was kept within these faded pages. He flicked through the pages again, noting certain entries with a deep pain in his heart.

Another anniversary- no trip again. Is it too much to want a vacation once a year? I would love to see Greece or Rome! The dinner was lovely, though, and Joe was so proud of the necklace he picked out. Sapphires. Imagine that? My Joe, picking sapphires for my neck, just like I'm royalty.

It's my birthday week. I'm hoping Joe picked up the cruise brochures I've been leaving out. I would love a cruise this summer. Only five days, surely, we can afford to get away for five days. See the islands. The girls at yoga would be so jealous.

Mother's day-Joe took me to see Ma again. She's getting worse. This is probably the last one. Joe picked up her favorite dinner and flowers on the way. He's always so thoughtful, even though she no longer remembers his name.

Christmas! Joe bought me a fur coat! Can you believe it? An actual fur. It's not a trip to Florida, but I'll take it. I just want to see the Keys one time. I heard it's beautiful there and the beaches. I just want to travel a little before I die. I'm not complaining about the fur, but I would love to see a beach again.

Page after page full of her small print, gifts, dates, memories, musings, failings, and that odd list in the back incriminating him more than anything ever had.

Joe finished his beer, stood up, and grabbed a fresh one from the fridge. He went into the small office off the kitchen and rummaged through Roxie's desk, looking for a notepad that he could use. He needed to make a list of his own. The drawers were filled with true crime magazines, maps, file folders, and other tidbits he had never wondered about before.

The desk was an office desk from a warehouse Joe had worked at in years ago. A beast of a thing with drawers on both sides. Roxie loved it and had filled it, and the room, with all manner of things, called it her office. Roxie spent hours here pouring over her crime files, cold cases, and missing person files; Joe used to tease her about playing armchair detective. Joe had never been able to find a thing in this room, let alone in the desk, but Roxie claimed she had a system. He returned to the table, found a clean page in his notebook, and flipped to the beginning of Roxie's.

Joe remained at the table for the rest of the night, writing and nursing one shitty beer after the other. He stopped when he heard a knock at the door around nine o'clock that night. Vinnie and Vito stood on the stoop holding a fresh pizza and a six-pack. Both wore matching velour lounge suits, Vinnie in maroon and Vito in gray. He let them in and resumed his task as the men made themselves at home, gathering paper plates, napkins, and the jar of red pepper flakes that Joe kept on the stove.

When they sat down across from Joe, he stopped his writing and accepted a plate of food from Vito. The trio ate in silence for a few minutes, no words needed as they consumed the steaming pie heaped with cheese, sauce, meats, and veggies. Vinnie broke the silence first, rocking back on his chair, and belching before pointing at the notebooks.

"What'cha working on, Joe?"

"A list," came Joe's quiet reply.

"What kind of list?" Vinnie asked, grabbing another slice from the box.

"A list of places that I need to see. Roxie had been keeping a list of things that she wanted to see and do, but I never noticed, never picked up on the clues. Or maybe I did, and I failed to act because I was too busy. She never complained, my Roxie. You guys know that, you were around. She never busted my balls. But this tiny notebook said it all. Breaking my heart to read it now, breaking my heart." Joe's voice cracked on a sob, and he trailed off.

"Roxie was a good woman, Joe. She loved you," Vito said, his low voice rumbling deep in his chest.

"What do you mean you need to see these places? What's the point of going now, without Roxie?" Vinnie asked, opening another beer.

"I gotta make it up to her," Joe said. "I'm going to take her ashes and scatter a little in each place on her list. I need to fix it, and this is the only way."

"That's a really nice way to honor your wife, Joe," Vito chimed in. "Anything we can do to help?"

"No thanks, fellas. I need to do this on my own."

"Sure, whatever you need, boss." They both stood and cleared the table of their small feast, piling the remaining slices on a plate for Joe for later. They tucked that and the last beer into the fridge.

"Maria sends her love. She wanted to make sure that you ate tonight," Vito told Joe, wrapping him in a bear hug before they turned to leave.

"Maria is a good girl, Vito. You should be proud of her. Good strong woman, just like I knew she would be."

Joe had helped them raise their little sister after their mom had died. The four of them had been thick as thieves, staying out of the eye and the reach of the state foster care system with Joe's crafty help.

His less than stellar aunt had shown him how to fake some papers at a young age, as she often left Joe on his own for weeks as she traipsed around the country with various men. School absence excuses, food stamp forms, doctors' notes; Joe could forge her name on anything. When Miss Magda Salvatore had passed away suddenly, Vinnie, Vito, and baby Maria were on the verge of being sent into foster care, when Joe's aunt stepped in to open her home to them. While she only saw more government money, Joe saw his best friends become his brothers.

The old brownstone duplex was passed to her care until the boys reached eighteen. The state issued checks to Joe's aunt, and the kids were left to their own devices most of the time, never even moving out of their side of the duplex. Instead, Joe, older by almost two years, moved into their side.

It was Joe who taught the boys how to make ramen noodles and hamburger helper. Joe showed them how to fix the formula for baby Maria and change her diapers. Joe taught them how to wash their clothes and how to forge school notes. Joe took baby Maria to her first day of school and bandaged her knees when she fell roller skating. Vinnie and Vito worshiped Joe and still did.

The Italian boys grew into twin beasts, large, stocky, and muscular, while Joe remained short and deceptively small. Joe could lift either one of the Italians up and slam them on their backs, and they both knew it. His rage far outdid his stature. It was Joe who ran their business, while the brothers were his wingmen.

Young Maria had a hell of a time when it came to dating. If her brothers were not scary enough, Joe's reputation preceded him. His piercing eyes would cut to your soul if you dared to disrespect the pretty girl he helped raise. He was more protective of her than anyone. He saw what disrespectful men did to his aunt on more than one occasion, and he would be damned if anyone treated baby Maria that way.

The three young men found work by the docks, in the strip, running games, running money, running girls, whatever the local mobsters had needed until Joe himself began quietly rising through the ranks, as more of their enemies quietly began to vanish. Soon, they had a fortune between them and went legit, mostly. Their hard work kept Maria off the streets and in the books, and her culinary degree had paid off.

Her restaurant was one of the best in the neighborhood. Her

brothers flipped houses for a living, amongst other things, and Joe kept a watchful eye over everything.

But someone else had been watching too. Roxie with her too big hair and piercing eyes that saw everything. Roxie and her damn list.

Joe bid the guys a goodnight and watched them go. Memories falling over each other like dominoes in his mind. They were good guys. He didn't need to involve them in this. He would take care of Roxie's list on his own.

CHAPTER THREE: TRAVEL PLANS

When morning came, Joe got up with a purpose. He had been up for hours the night before, compiling the list for his travel needs.

He would honor his wife with her greatest unspoken wishes and take her abroad. Better late than never. His heart was heavy with mourning, but he felt settled and resolved today. He had a plan. Joe thrived on plans and organization, to the point of obsession.

He was supremely proud of his patience in every area of his life, and it had served him well. Patience kept him and the boys out of juvie and jail. Patience kept him from making small mistakes over years of dirty deeds. He took his time planning his trips, his jobs, and his business, double and triple checking for mistakes, accidents, and errors.

Joe went through his morning routine, unhurried as usual, with coffee at hand, and the laptop beside him. He began to plan his trip. When his travel agent called. Notes were exchanged, and phone calls ended. Joe did his part of the planning. His agent would handle the rest.

Shortly after 1:30, the fellas dropped by with his lunch. Homemade lasagna from Maria's, house salad, and garlic toast. His traditional slice of cheesecake was packaged separately so it would stay chilled. They ate as Joe filled them in on his. He was not concerned about being away from the house. The entire neighborhood knew not to mess with Joe's house. Business was discussed, contractors vetted, bids accepted. Vinnie and Vito had their assignments. Joe had his.

After lunch, Joe went to the bank, and the corner drugstore, then home to pack. As expected, his itinerary was on the printer in the small office, and he set it on the table with his keys, passport, wallet, and cell phone. Upstairs to the bathroom and tiny hall closet to pack his small toiletry kit. Back to the bedroom to pack one small travel bag with essentials. He would buy anything else he might need along the way. He found clothing disposable, like most other things.

Bag in hand, he headed downstairs to the kitchen. His leather carry-on held several items: two novels, a well-read Clive Barker and an equally dog-eared Edward Lee, and Roxie's notepad. His itinerary was tucked into a plastic folder. The small box containing a few ounces of Roxie's ashes, carefully sealed and packed by the funeral home, with a note tucked away with it for customs and security.

By three o'clock, he was on his way to JFK, escorted by Vito and Vinnie.

CHAPTER FOUR: ABROAD WITHOUT HIS BROAD.

Joe landed in Greece, twenty-four hours later, exhausted, but glad to be on solid ground.

Another leg of his journey took him to the port in Volos and then a ferry ride to the island. The waiting driver quickly gathered his bags and deposited Joe at the five-star hotel, situated on a hillside overlooking the sparkling turquoise of the ocean and white, sandy beaches. The suite was plush and beautifully appointed, and his dinner, a delectable spread of souvlaki with a side of tzatziki and fresh bread, was served to him within thirty minutes. An attendant took his suits to be pressed and left Joe on the balcony with a bottle of champagne and his thoughts.

The small box of ashes sat on the table just inside the open doors and Joe toasted his late wife with a tear in his eye. He muttered his apologies and his love through his misty eyes as he stood up, watching the sea as the waves came rolling in, crashing on the shore, white foam curling up from the clear blue surf. Miles of trees covered the rolling hills that surrounded the beachfront, leaves of emerald and jade whispering in the salty breeze.

The stone buildings looked like they had been carved right out of the seaside cliffs, hues of beige, tan, and white, kissed by terra cotta and sunshine. Understated luxury was everywhere, blending in with the small town filled with residents and summer tourists. Boutique stores lined the streets in front of the hotels and bistros, exquisite artisan shops selling handmade wares, and gourmet eateries. The town dripped with color, warmth, and wine.

"You would have loved it, Roxie. It's gorgeous here, truly gorgeous." His voice cracked a bit as he turned away and stepped back inside.

No time like the present to do what he was here to do. He carefully picked up the small box and opened it, pulling out a small bag full of grainy filaments, all that remained of his beloved, reduced to charred bits of bone. The box contained ten matching pouches, each carrying an ounce of his heart. He slipped the pouch in his pocket and set the box down, covered and secured once more.

He rang the concierge for his driver, slipped on his sports coat, and made his way to the lobby to wait. Barely five minutes later, a sleek BMW appeared in front of the doors. Joe went out to meet the driver, who waited by his open door. After giving him an address, Joe slid inside and settled on the butter-soft leather seat. It reminded him of Roxie's skin, velvet-soft and extra-tanned. His lips lifted in a rueful grin; he always did get on her about going to those tanning salons so much.

"Gonna turn into leather. You keep going to that salon," Joe used to say, grinning when Roxie would try to take a swipe at him with one of her true crime magazines. "*Gotta get my color somehow, Joe. You hate the beach.*" Roxie would shoot back, her voice high and nasal. She would chase him from the room, shooing him away and he would laugh at her faked annoyance. All for laughs, she was good for a laugh, his Roxie.

The shades over his eyes failed to conceal the lone tear that slowly trickled down his weathered face. Soft music filtered through the speakers as he rode in the otherwise silent car, the powerful machine cutting through the winding roads with ease, taking him to the beach that his love had so longed to see. She had loved the musical, Mama Mia, and often talked about visiting the small island it had been filmed on, Skopelos. He had asked the driver to take him to the quietest beach on the island. He did not wish to be disturbed while saying goodbye to his Roxie.

He leaned his head back for a moment, fatigue suddenly hitting him. The trip had been long, and he ached for a bed, but he would not make Roxie wait any longer; he was already too late.

He could hear the waves crashing on the beach as they drove. Small dunes rose around the car, dotted with bright green grasses and a myriad of wildflowers.

Soon, they pulled into a wide parking area. The white sand stretched out before the vehicle, sparkling in the fading sun as it began to descend across the horizon. The driver, Antonio, quickly hopped out and opened the passenger door with a slight flourish.

"Thank you, Antonio," Joe said quietly, removing his dark glasses and gazing at the water, sparkling like the sapphires he had given to Roxie on their anniversary. Vibrant bushes and shrubs covered the sloping hills that rose all around them, almost hiding the beach from the town above. The water rolled in, hypnotic in both motion and sound as it crashed, broke, and receded, then repeated the cycle.

"Take your time, sir. The sun sets in twenty minutes and the town lights will come on shortly. I'll remain here with the car. There is a small cooler of drinks in the trunk if you would like to take something with you? Champagne, wine, water?"

"No, thank you. I'm fine for now. I will see you when I return." Joe began walking along the path, one hand gently closed over the small pouch in his pocket. His heart ached, but he would see this promise fulfilled.

~

JOE MADE HIS WAY CLOSE TO THE WATER'S EDGE, SLIPPED OFF HIS LOAFERS, rolled his pant legs up, and slid the small bag from his pocket. Holding it, he began to walk into the surf. The clear water showed a soft sandy bottom where small rocks and bits of shell glistened; curly tendrils of seaweed rubbed against his ankles as he trudged along, talking to Roxie as he did so.

"Well, we're here, Rox. Right on the beach where they filmed the movie, right here where your favorite actress sang and danced. Right here, where I never bothered to take you while you were alive and full of life." He trailed off, composing himself for a moment before he continued, "I'm so sorry, Roxie. I've been so selfish, so close-minded. I never knew how much you longed to see the world. I found your notebook; I guess you know that now, or we wouldn't be here." He took a moment to clear his throat, clearing the lump that lingered there.

"I'm going to fix it, Rox, fix all of it. You'll see. I'll make it right. I'm going to track them all down, every one of them. You found them for me, baby. You always said you would. I'm sorry I never took you seriously, never thought of you as a partner in this life of mine. Guess I thought I was protecting you, but it was you, wasn't it, sweetheart? You were the one protecting us all along."

Joe finally let a tear drop from his misty eyes as he opened the small pouch and poured the gray ashes into his palm. He bent forward and, with a soft blow from his pursed lips, the ashes fanned out into the sea.

"You can rest now, love. Here in the sea, where you'll always carry a piece of me. Goodbye, my wife, you were the best part of me." His tears dropped gently into the waves as the particles floated away. He backed away a few feet, watching as the ashes ebbed to and fro, cradled on the surf, like a mother rocking a babe. He watched until he could no longer see the ashes and the water began to glow like molten gold. Finally, he turned, with dry eyes, and headed back to the beach, and the car beyond.

Antonio stood waiting, as Joe seated himself inside the car. The driver held out a bottle of chilled water when he was settled. Joe accepted it wordlessly, twisted the cap off, and drank half of it in one long draught.

"Back to the hotel, please, Antonio. And thank you for the water." Joe spoke quietly and offered the man a small smile, genuine and grateful.

"You are quite welcome, sir. The heat does get intense here," Antonio replied, closed the door, made his way around to the driver's seat, and began the short drive back to the hotel.

When he reached his suite that night, Joe took a long shower and sat on the balcony with a glass of chilled Ouzo, a favorite local drink. Finally, he made his way to bed, exhaustion easing his chaotic thoughts and the alcohol blurring his grief just enough for him to rest.

CHAPTER FIVE: A GARROTING IN GLOSSA

He woke promptly at seven fifteen, rang for his breakfast, and began getting ready for the day. His meal arrived right on time, and he ushered the server in, gave the young man a generous tip, and sat down to eat. The food was delicious; a beautiful omelet overflowing with vegetables, a side of fresh fruit and pastry, dark roast coffee, and a Bloody Mary.

He spent a few minutes on the balcony, gazing at the horizon, wanting to etch its beauty into his memory. Regret washed over him once more as he realized just how much he had missed out on by not bringing Roxie on trips like this one. She deserved the world, and he never gave it to her; he thought he had. He really did. He adored her, but he had missed the signs of her discontentment.

Inside, he picked up his bag and called the driver; he had another stop to make before he caught his ferry to the mainland.

Joe slid inside the car after handing the driver his suitcase and put his briefcase beside him. He sat back and focused his mind on the task at hand, recalling the details from Roxie's list that he had saved on his phone.

Joe gave Antonio the address and rode silently as they left the small town behind. An hour later, the black sedan pulled up slowly to the small village of Glossa, high in the hills. Joe gave the driver a few bills to go inside the nearest bistro for a coffee, advising him to take his time. He would be gone for a while to do some sightseeing. Antonio reminded him that he needed to be at the port for the ferry by two o'clock that afternoon to catch his flight on time; Joe assured him he would return by then and set off.

The town was ripe with activity and Joe easily lost himself in the chaos, with tourists eager to see the village, sample the food, and over-indulge in the local spirits. The day was full of sunshine, and heat emanated off the streets and buildings around him, washing over him like a blanket, thick and stifling. He casually walked the length of the main street, entered several shops, buying colorful trinkets as he went, then continued to the end of the lane and vanished around the corner.

Twenty minutes of walking through the cobbled streets led him deeper into the village to the quiet section of residential homes. Soon, he found the address he was looking for and studied the small house from across the street. He continued around the block, observing all he passed, and finding nothing of concern, he made a second pass of the house, this time from the narrow alley running between the backs of the homes.

A courtyard framed by a waist-high iron fence set off the rear of the house. An old statue stood empty in the middle, devoid of water, and streaked with grime. The grass was short and well-kept, and small plants bordered the path. The house looked quiet, but he could hear the sounds of a television inside or perhaps a radio. The back door stood open, leaving only the screened door to contend with. Joe would bet a dollar to a donkey that it was unlocked.

He sauntered down the walk and opened the small gate as if he was expected and walked through the courtyard to the inviting door; it was unlocked. He slipped inside, careful to hold the door so it wouldn't slam into the frame, and listened for any movement from the house. The silence held, so he turned and closed the back door, locking it against any other visitors.

He set his briefcase down next to his other purchases beside the door, then unzipped the side pocket and donned a pair of long latex gloves.

The kitchen held a small table and chairs, a sink full of dirty dishes, and a stove covered with takeout boxes. The floor looked like it hadn't seen a mop in a decade. Joe shook his head at the mess and walked through the archway into the next room.

A glance showed it was empty except for a television on a carved wooden stand, a couch, and two chairs, both covered in an orange color that matched the rug on the floor. Sheer but dingy white curtains hung in long swags over the windows, and several vases sat in a cobweb-covered corner, filled with dried grasses and feathers. He heard a sound coming from upstairs, music and elevated voices, a commercial most likely, a grunt, and then heavy footsteps.

Joe paused next to the stairs, waiting to see where the person would go. A door opened, then came the unmistakable sound of a man urinating in a toilet, the heavy stream splashing into the water like a waterfall. Joe grinned sardonically, sounded like an afternoon bender piss to him. Perfect timing on his part. He began to slide his belt from his pants.

He mounted the stairs, his belt in his hands. Without a sound, he stepped into the small bathroom right behind the large man in a most compromising position.

Joe raised his arms and wrapped the belt around the man's neck before he could form words. A startled yell began and then vanished as the belt quickly cut off his oxygen. Joe pressed down on the buckle with his thumb and a thin razor wire released from the belt seam. With a firm sawing motion, then a backward tug on both ends, the wire sliced through Roberto Santini's neck with a sickening meaty rip. A geyser of blood shot out as Roberto met Joe's eyes in the bathroom mirror, his legs propelling him back as his arms flailed and thrashed at Joe's hands, trying, and failing, to stop the assault.

Joe grinned in response to the man's expression as blood splattered on his glasses and face, then began coating the walls and pouring down over Roberto's shirt, enormous gut, and flaccid penis. Roberto's eyes grew wide with shock, followed by recognition, then nothing, as the life faded from them. Joe let go and shoved the man forward into the tub. The shower curtain rings popped as the heavy man collapsed, taking the plastic sheeting with him. Blood flowed like a river.

Joe looked at the man with the satisfied look of a job well done on his face and he had Roxie to thank for it.

He and the boys had been looking for this crook for years, ever since he stiffed them on a contracting job. Roberto had vanished, owing them a hundred grand, plus interest. Joe had extracted some of the debt from Roberto's partner, but Santini had already skipped town by the time Joe had come for him.

The first entry on Roxie's list had read *"Mama Mia Island (Skopelos). 31081 Haag Keys, Glossa"*, all printed in her neat script. When he found the matching file folder for the island, all the information Roxie had tracked down on Santini was there, photos, bank accounts, known aliases; everything Joe would need to settle a long overdue score. He had been stunned at what else the files had held.

Pictures of Roberto with young girls caged and chained. Bank statements for offshore accounts. Lists of illicit goods imported and exported, including drugs, women, and children. Roberto had his fingers in everything.

Joe stepped over to the sink and turned the faucet on, stripping out of his shirt, pants, and shoes. He grabbed a towel from the rack and began washing the scarlet stains from his gloved hands, face, and neck. When he finished, he padded down the steps and retrieved his briefcase from the kitchen floor, where he set it. Bag in hand, he went back upstairs and found Roberto's bedroom, littered with more takeout boxes and empty beer bottles. Disgusted, he swept the filth from a corner of the bed and unzipped the hidden bottom of the bag.

He pulled out a sealed packet, tore it open, and unfolded it. Then he began patting down the bed, floor, and hallway, scouring any area he had been for loose hairs or fibers; the heavy adhesive square was able to pick up an eyelash or a grain of sand. A second pass was made of the bathroom area, especially the area around the sink. Concentrated bleach wipes came out next, and he used them to cleanse the heavy latex gloves of all traces of blood, saving one to wipe the door handles on his way out.

He removed his ruined clothes and put on a fresh set, exact matches to the clothes he had been wearing. Next, he took out a thin square of plastic, unfolded it, and opened it. His bloody clothes went into this bag along with the adhesive squares and gloves. He sealed the bag, rolled it tight, and placed it back inside the false bottom. Placing his shades back on, he slung his briefcase over his shoulder and headed back down the steps.

He began to whistle as he picked up his shopping bags, adjusted his glasses, and stepped outside, casually wiping the door handle as he went. Joe left the courtyard, a tourist out for a stroll in the midday sunshine. He made his way back to the small cafe where Antonio sat at a small table on the patio, sipping a cold drink, and watching a group of pretty girls giggling over their lunch. Joe lifted a hand to get his attention, and the driver swiftly rose from his seat and headed to the car.

"All set, sir?" he asked, quickly taking the packages and opening the door.

"Yes, we can go to the port now," Joe replied as he got inside. Antonio started the car and Joe watched the hills and the coast fade away as they drove towards the port to the mainland.

CHAPTER SIX: AN OLD MAN IN THE OLD COUNTRY

By early evening, Joe found himself in Italy, just outside of Milan, in a small village called Crema.

His room at the di Sant' Anna was spotless, furnished with tasteful antiques and quality woods that gleamed in the light. He opened the curtains and allowed the sunset to flood his room in a golden glow. The warm apricot streaks fell across the walls and reminded him of the delicate rose petals on Roxie's casket at the funeral parlor. He made a mental note to call Vito and remind him to water the rose bushes behind the house. He didn't want them to wither and die. He would keep Roxie's roses blooming until the day he died. It was all he had left of her, that, and the small box of ashes that he carried with him.

Italy had long been on her list, mentioned multiple times as he read through the worn notebook. Vatican City, Milan, Rome, all the beautiful places that she had read about and had seen in her Lifetime movies. The art museums, the sheer grace of the buildings, works of art in and of themselves, the history that the old country was soaked in like blood across the battlefield.

He had rented a car in Milan and planned to drive through Florence and on to Rome, stopping for a couple of hours in each place to take in the sights that Roxie no longer could. His trip would end with the scattering of her ashes on the grounds of the Colosseum. He lifted the small box that held her ashes and took one of the sealed packets out. He slid it into his pocket, wanting to keep it close to him, and slid on his jacket to find dinner.

A short drive took him to a small restaurant highly recommended by the hotel staff. It was small but filled to capacity. Lanterns hung everywhere, inside and out, lighting the patio with a soft ambiance. Flowering vines cascaded down the sides of the building and bordered the stone wall around the plaza. A gorgeous marble statue of the Virgin and child stood in the center of it, water gurgling as it cascaded from the seven carved spouts. Blue glass stones filled the wide basin, catching the lights and making them dance across the ripples.

He seated himself in the far corner of the patio, facing the street; this table allowed him the chance to watch both the people eating and those walking by. A pretty waitress with deep green eyes and hair wrought from flames sauntered over with a friendly smile. Her black slacks were crisply pressed, and her white blouse hugged her frame and her curves. A bright scarf hung loosely around her neck, like a shawl, and knotted in front. A single gold necklace, bearing a gold cross, dangled just above her collarbone. The pretty girl reminded him so much of a young Maria, so much so that it made his heart ache.

"Welcome to the Familia Ristorante. What may I bring you tonight?" she smiled and waited patiently as he glanced at the menu.

"You know what?" Joe said, slowly setting the menu down. "How about you bring me the best dishes on the menu tonight? One of everything, soup, salad, starter, the works. Whatever the chef recommends."

"Big appetite tonight?" she asked.

"Well, I am here celebrating my Roxie, my recently departed Roxie, and Italy is our blood, our heritage, and she never got the chance to see it. She would have wanted to taste everything, see everything." Joe removed his dark glasses and smiled sadly at the waitress. "Since she no longer can, I am going to do it for her, then tell her all about it in my dreams."

"I'm so sorry to hear that. What a heavy loss you carry. That is a beautiful way to honor her memory." She reached out, squeezed his hand gently, in the way a daughter might, and left to go inside. "I'll be back shortly."

His Roxie would have raved over each inch of this place. The candles flickered in the soft breeze, and the sky was clear overhead, giving way to a light show that only nature could as stars shone above, twinkling in the abyss of space. The trickling water of the fountain added another layer to the soundtrack of soft classical music that was playing inside the restaurant. Artwork hung on every available space, and a bright mural of Vatican City was painted on the outer wall facing the patio.

He wiped his glasses with the soft linen napkin and glanced up as the waitress approached with a small tray of drinks. A carafe of sangria and a clean glass were placed in front of him, with a bottle of chilled San Benedetto water and a trim flute of champagne. A bowl of oil and vinegar with bread for dipping joined the group, and a small cheese board crowded with olives, meats, and cheeses.

"Thank you," he said with a smile, as he looked at the food before him. He truly was hungry, and his stomach chose that moment to rumble.

Joe began to eat, sampling small bites from each platter, thoroughly enjoying the full flavors that exploded on his tongue. He had barely gotten started when the young lady was back with a house salad, brimming with garden vegetables and a covered bowl that he discovered held minestrone.

The next course she brought out contained a bowl of traditional Tortelli Cremaschi, a pasta dish containing dough pillows filled with cocoa amaretti, mastaccino biscuit with spices, raisins, dry anise liquor, candied lemon, mint, and Grana Padano cheese. Full to bursting, Joe almost groaned when she appeared with his coffee and dessert, a thick slice of Torta Bertolina. The decadent cake was chock full of Concord grapes and smelled amazing.

The food was exquisite and rich; the wine was just sweet enough to complement the full meal, and his waitress had been beyond competent. She cheerfully packed each unfinished portion of his meal into boxes for him to take back to his hotel and added a small glass bottle of their sangria to his bag.

Joe paid her and tipped her abundantly well, then began the short drive to his rental. Once back at the hotel, the staff graciously took his meal to the kitchen to be stored. Joe took a walk around the grounds, with only his small briefcase on his shoulder, hands thrust deep in his pockets, just taking in the quiet night, wanting to capture it in his memory so he could tell Roxie about it later that night before he showed her in his dreams. His right thumb stroked the small packet of Roxie's ashes as he went, tracing the small remains of his love, ashen and gray like his soul.

He ventured through the courtyard, admiring the statues and fountains, the many topiaries, and manicured hedges as he wandered. The pathway was lit with glowing amber solar lights and smooth stones led the way through the gardens; it was truly a breathtaking sight to behold, night or day. His steps took him to the back corner of the lush lawn, and he slipped out of the gate, vanishing into the night.

~

JOE ENDED HIS WALK HALFWAY ACROSS THE SMALL TOWN, WHERE HE STOOD gazing up at the veranda of a small house. Music drifted from the open window and laughter spilled out into the night. It sat alone on the corner, beige stone, and tiled roof, blending in with the others. Joe knew the back would hold a postage stamp square of lawn, a fountain of some sort, or perhaps a statue, overrun with weeds or shrubs that hadn't been trimmed. No roses would bloom here, no neat hedges to border the fence with a proud line of lush green.

He knew the iron fence would creak when it opened, and he knew the back door would be locked. Benny "Cyclops" Castellano was paranoid and a slob, and when he ran, he had run to the old country, hoping the heart of Italy would protect one of its own. Old Cyclops in there had Vinnie and Vito to thank for his missing left eye. A heated poker game at the pool hall had turned ugly and before Benny could run from the fight, Vito had run a pool stick clean through his eye socket, the eye had popped out the same time the pool cue had, dangling wetly on Benny's cheek as blood gushed from the ruined flesh around it.

As Benny screamed in horror, in a pitch a soprano would have been proud of, Vinnie had reached up and yanked the orbit from the tendril that it clung to and threw it across the room.

"That'll teach you to side-eye me, you old bastard! You lousy cheat!" Vinnie had roared in his face, his massive hands slamming into the screaming man's chest, pushing Benny clear across the table in one thrust. Poker chips and cards sprayed everywhere as Benny landed on his ass, clutching at his eye, the screams never halting from his lips. Snot and drool ran down his face, mixing with the blood that coated the left side of his face, chin, and neck and slid wetly down to his shirt collar. Vito had followed up the attack with a good clobbering until the police sirens forced them to split. Benny, to his one and only credit, did not snitch but instead chose to run.

Joe hated a coward, but he hated a cheat even more. Benny owed them five hundred large and the deed to his properties in the Bronx. Joe no longer cared about the money or the deeds. He had made ten times that in the years since. What Joe cared about now was the principle of the thing. No one made a fool out of Joe Marshall.

Joe watched as the lights dimmed and the music lessened in volume. Reaching into the side pocket of his bag, he removed a pair of gloves and slipped them on as he rounded the house. Everything was just as he assumed: statues, no fountain, overgrown weeds crawling up the sides of the fence. An overturned trash can was tossed just beyond the door and both rear windows were open. The side door was just ahead of Joe. He decided to try that entrance first.

The narrow walkway conveniently hid him in shadow as he tested the door, but it was locked. He took out a slim tool from his briefcase and slid it into the door frame, wiggling the knob slightly as he did so, then he felt the mechanism give way. He smiled as he let himself in, locking the door behind him. He stood in a small, tiled hallway that led to the kitchen and another room lay just beyond it. A closed door stood beside him and one more just ahead.

He quickly checked both doors, finding a powder room, a small closet that held cleaning supplies, and an overflowing trash can that reeked of rotting food. Joe continued down the hallway, barely sparing a glance at the filthy kitchen before checking the darkened sitting room. All empty but music and low voices could be heard overhead. He set the leather briefcase down on the chair closest to him and took out the one item he would need, his custom-made ebony pool stick.

He slid the slim case from the false bottom and began to screw two of the pieces together. When he finished, he slipped his loafers off and began to stalk his prey, which sat unaware, somewhere above him. As he reached the top of the stairs, a hallway opened on his right, 3 doors ran the length of it: a bathroom, a closed door, and a door, slightly ajar, at the end. This must be the bedroom, Joe thought, seeing as it faced the front street and the veranda he had been watching from outside. He crept toward the far door, moving with a purpose, pool cue in hand. His eyes darkened to a stormy blue and his heartbeat pulsed, calm and steady.

Right outside the door, he could see Benny lounging on the bed, focused on the television. Music drifted from a speaker on the bedside table, surrounded by empty wine bottles. Joe pushed the door open with the pool stick and strode to the bedside before Benny could blink his good eye. Joe had the wooden rod under his chin, pinning him to the headboard by the time Benny croaked out his name.

"Joe, wait, let me explain," Benny wheezed. His face grew redder by the second and his one eye was wide with shock and fright.

"Explain? It's too late to explain, Benny old boy," Joe said calmly, his voice taut with venom. "You had years to make it right. Years when you could have sent the money, or the deeds, or come to me like a man. I'm a patient man, Benny, a reasonable man."

"Give me some time! I can get the money, please!" Benny begged, tears trickling from one eye. His arms grasped the stick, trying to pull it away, but Joe was much stronger than Benny had ever been.

Joe looked at him for a moment, then began to nod and stepped back. Both hands grasped the stick as Benny gasped and rubbed his neck, turning to sit on the edge of the bed, right where Joe wanted him.

"I swear, I can get it, twenty-four hours, and it's yours. The deeds, the money, all of it," Benny rasped, still rubbing his neck.

"Sorry, but your time is up," Joe said with a shrug, then lunged at Benny with the ebony stick, releasing the razor blade on the tip as he did so, jamming it into Benny's eye and twisting it in deep.

Benny fell back on the bed, screaming as blood gushed down his face. Joe thrust the stick again, ramming it into his throat and yanking it across his neck, cutting off the scream in one sudden motion. Blood poured out of the neck wound, flowing down both sides of his neck, gurgling sounds issued from Benny as he lay twitching on the bed, blind and dying. Joe Marshall had kept his promise and made sure he was the last thing Benny ever saw.

Joe stepped back and withdrew the pool stick, wiping the blood and bits of ruined flesh on the duvet. He began to whistle as he left the room, retrieved his bag, and began his clean-up. Roxie had done him proud. She had been a true crime buff and an armchair sleuth her whole life, but he never realized the depth of her true talents.

She loved to watch true crime documentaries. She would take notes and start investigating unsolved crimes on her own, telling Joe it kept her mind sharp. He indulged her adventures, anything to keep her happy, but Roxie had stepped up her investigating skills. The back of her notebook had been filled with notes on the handful of men that had done Joe and the boys dirty, scum that had skipped out their debts, putting Joe's business in a perilous situation, and that one dirtbag that had assaulted Maria as she was leaving her restaurant. Joe was saving that one for last.

Roxie had spent the last several years tracking each man down, noting their movements, tracking bank accounts, and routines. It was all in her notebook, all secreted away in her chaotic office, hidden in plain sight. Benny's entry had read "*Crema, Italy, 172 Contrada lole.*" The matching folder held every detail of Benny's life in the old country. Government corruption, running drugs, cars and women, nothing was off-limits for this low life. There was no job too filthy for Benny, nothing too vile. Roxie had proof of it all, from receipts to bank accounts, incriminating pictures and government names that ran all the way to the top. Joe already sent that little tidbit of info to Interpol anonymously.

Joe smiled warmly, thinking of Roxie's final gift to him, and looked over at Benny once more. Bodily fluids stained the bed, and rivers of putrid stool leaked down his legs. His ratty bathrobe hung open over his sweat-stained t-shirt and boxers. Old Benny "Cyclops" Castellano was finito. Joe finished changing his clothes, packed up his pool stick, and left the room, walked downstairs, and left the house, locked up and silent, except for the canned laughter blaring from the television.

∿

THE NEXT DAY, JOE DROVE FROM MILAN INTO FLORENCE, VISITING SEVERAL vineyards along the way, leaving a bit of Roxie scattered across the grounds of the prettiest one. He sampled the wines, sent a case home to remember her by, and continued his journey to Rome. He spent the evening there, seeing the sights, marveling at so much beauty in one place, and left part of his beloved on the blood-soaked ruins of the Colosseum.

He spent an hour there, softly describing it to his wife, imagining that she could hear him, hoping she could. He could almost feel the power the massive arena once held. As the sunset, he made his way to the museums, taking Roxie to the Sistine Chapel, and through St. Peter's Basilica. He spent the night in a penthouse suite and left for Spain early the next morning, ready for the next leg of Roxie's trip.

CHAPTER SEVEN: MADRID AND A MURDER

Joe arrived in Madrid refreshed and recharged, despite the grueling hours of his trip so far; traveling from place to place in such a short time frame would have taken its toll on a normal person, but Joe was not quite your average Joe.

He unpacked in his suite, meticulous in his precision, then packed his briefcase once more with his usual supplies for the evening. The first stop for him would be The Royal Palace and the gardens for his Roxie, then dinner.

Roxie's notes for Salvatore Santoni were saturated with the man's routines and foul business dealings, sex trafficking, and kiddie porn among them. He had already made quite a name for himself with the local thugs. Joe would be doing them and the world a favor. He loathed men who harmed the innocent. He checked the notes on his phone again, *"Madrid-Flamenco Moreria, VA103 Castile & Leon"*, made a note of the address, and headed for a shower. Finished, dressed, and ready for his night, he headed out into the warm sun, a pocketful of Roxie and a soul full of rage.

The Royal Palace tour had been glorious, and Joe loved the incredible beauty of the gardens. Everywhere he looked, he only saw the sights that his Roxie was missing. His heart ached as he lovingly described every detail to his beloved, the packet in his pocket growing warm under his touch, as his thumb rubbed and stroked the smooth plastic, feeling the coarse bits of ash under his touch. He took a quiet moment near a magnificent flowerbed of white lilies and gently sprinkled Roxie's ashes into his palm, then blew it out over the delicate petals. A single tear dropped in the grass as he said a fresh goodbye.

Two hours later, Joe headed into the warm evening, dark suit freshly pressed, gold cufflinks gleaming under the streetlights, shoes shining from a fresh polish. The Flamenco restaurant was the highest rated in the city and on Roxie's list of places to see. Santoni also happened to be a frequent flier. Joe hoped for dinner and a show. He began to whistle as he quickened his step, eager to sample the local flavor.

Joe reached the restaurant in a few minutes and slowed his pace, scanning the crowded sidewalk as couples flowed in and out of the bar. The area was bustling with activity, sleek cars lingered at the curb, taxis sat idling in the street unloading passengers, scooters, and pedestrians all passing by on their way to home, bars, or food. He made his way to the entrance and was quickly seated by a gorgeous woman. She led him to a quiet table near the stage but in a dark corner as asked.

He could see the door, the corridor leading to the kitchen, and the performance stage. Perfect view of everything. He ordered drinks and a starter from the waitress and sat back, patient and comfortable. When the drinks arrived, he ordered sea bass with roasted vegetables and house salad, then added cheesecake for his dessert. The food began to arrive just before the house lights dimmed and the curtains parted.

The venue was packed; the show was wildly entertaining and exhilarating. Joe almost felt the urge to dance. He watched, appreciative of the sensual movements of the dancers, the grace and elegance of the dance, and the chaotic frenzy that took over when the tempo increased. Roxie would have been enraptured throughout the performance. But something else had kept his attention during the latter half.

Santoni entered the bar thirty minutes into the show. Joe spotted him immediately. The slicked back, combed over hair was a dead giveaway, as were the chunky gold rings and black silk shirt open at the collar to display his gaudy gold cross. His burgundy suit clashed with the vibe of the whole venue. He watched him schmooze his way across the bar before settling next to a pretty young woman who seemed to be alone. Joe chuckled as she smacked his hand away when he tried to rest one hand on her rear, attempting to appear casual. She stood up and left, leaving Salvatore glaring after her and glancing around to see if anyone had noticed her rebuff.

The older man straightened his collar and waved the barkeep over for a drink. Joe would guarantee it was scotch, Sal's drink of choice. He kept watch as Sal downed drink after drink, trying and failing to hit on every woman who walked past him. Finally, he stood up and headed towards the men's room at the end of the hall. Joe waited a minute, then did the same.

As he entered the dimly lit room, Sal stood at the urinal, one hand on the wall as he drunkenly pissed, muttering to himself when he splashed the wall, then his shoes. He never even looked up as Joe entered. Joe stepped up to the urinal beside him, fumbled with his belt, pretending to be just as drunk, and stumbled slightly to his right, leaning into Sal, and depressing a button on his cufflink at the same time, then pressing his wrist against Sal's neck as he pretended to regain his balance.

"Ow, what the fuck you doing, you prick? Get off me!" Sal slurred, slapping Joe's hand before he resumed muttering and yanking up his fly, glaring at Joe as he did so.

"Sorry, old chap, sorry, bit too much to drink," Joe slurred back, relieving himself and watching Sal carefully in his peripheral vision. The old man staggered back a few steps, turned to the sink, then crumbled to the floor, vomit issuing from his mouth in a bloody stream as he went down. His cufflink held a tetrodotoxin filled needle, one of the most potent toxins known to man. The highly concentrated dose was fast acting and caused death in minutes.

Joe had paid a hefty price for his cufflinks to be outfitted with the poison needles, and it had been worth it. He quit the drunk act, fixed his pants, and locked the door. Then stood watching as Sal began to convulse on the floor. Blood began to seep from his nose and eyes as he spasmed violently on the ceramic tile. The stench of hot feces filled the air as Sal shit himself, moaning incoherently as his insides seized and his legs thrashed. Foamy drool, tinged pink, spilled from his lips as his head jerked from side to side. The pool of brackish fluid under him began to spread, as he spasmed once more, arcing off the floor as his body went rigid, then collapsed and lay still.

Joe took his glasses off and bent down to check him, soft leather gloves covering his hands. No pulse, no heartbeat. Burst blood vessels had turned both eyes crimson and blood leaked from his ears. Joe stood up, straightened his jacket, and unlocked the door. He

stepped out into the dark corridor. The frantic tones of the finale
filled the air, the music pulsed in time with the swirling lights. Joe
slid back into his seat, finished his wine, and stood for the ovation as
the curtain fell.

~

JOE SAUNTERED FROM THE CLUB, ENJOYING THE NIGHT AIR, RELISHING THE
chaos as Sal's body had been discovered and the club had been evac-
uated. Joe blended in with the crowd, chatting with a few couples as
they raved over the dance and the food. At the corner, he bid them a
goodnight and continued on to his hotel. An hour later, he was
seated on the balcony, sipping on a fine bottle of merlot, and telling
his angel all about his night.

In the morning, Joe arrived at the airport right on time. His flight
to Vegas boarded in an hour. He checked into the first-class lounge,
ordered breakfast and coffee, and settled in to wait. As he ate, he sent
a single message to Vinnie and Vito. When the plane boarded, Joe
settled into his seat, briefcase at his feet, Roxie nestled right on top,
and a smile of contentment on his face.

CHAPTER EIGHT: TEARS OF A CLOWN

By eight o'clock that evening, he was checking into another penthouse suite in his favorite casino, escorted by Vinnie and Vito. The
friends spent the evening going over the events of Joe's trip, followed
by food and gambling in the casino. At midnight, the three lifelong
friends made one more trip to an address on Roxie's list. *"Vegas-
Circus Circus-Night Act"*. The file that Joe had found marked *"Vegas"*
was the most important gift Roxie could have left for him, but he
knew it was meant for all of them.

Five years ago, Maria had been assaulted as she was closing for
the night. When she went to the back entry to set the alarm, she had
opened it to check outside, and a man had burst in. A greasy rat-face

man from the neighborhood called Weasel. He leered at her and lunged, grabbing her by the hair and slamming her face into the steel prep table. He had thrown her to the floor, kicking her several times before he grabbed her, and tried to lay her out on the table.

Vinnie had come inside looking for her when Maria did not come to the car after setting the alarm. He heard her screaming and found Weasel ripping Maria's pants down. He had knocked the man senseless before rushing to help his sister. Vinnie had rushed her to the hospital for the injuries to her face and had called Joe and Vito on the way. They searched for Weasel for days, but he had vanished. Maria recovered, but was never the same. The haunted look in her eyes every time she heard a loud sound was heartbreaking. She could not be left alone anymore and had moved back in with her brothers. Weasel had not only broken her ribs, but he had also broken her spirit.

The trio made their way to the Circus Circus casino and sat waiting in a bar across the street. Roxie had tracked Weasel here, working as a clown for the famous casino. Drunk during the day, perverted Bozo at night. An hour later, a ragged half-dressed clown came shuffling out of the casino, face paint smeared, wig gone, oversized shoes clutched in one hand. Weasel looked every inch of a meth-head as he stumbled down the sidewalk. Vinnie and Vito stood up first, leaving the bar to follow him on their side of the street.

Joe paid the tab, left, and crossed the street, following behind the strung-out clown. Weasel never glanced up, never looked across the street. He barely acknowledged the traffic lights or crossing signals. He wove across blocks, stumbling and cursing, yelling at people that got in his way before finally turning into a half-empty parking lot in front of a shitty motel. They watched as he dragged himself up the stairs and into room 301.

Minutes later, Joe opened the door that Weasel had been too high to remember to lock, and the four men stood staring at each other. Weasel was on the bed, beer in hand. The brothers loomed on either side of him and Joe in the middle, his piercing blue eyes breaking the man's soul. A low whimper began to fill the room as the clown began to back-peddle across the bed, falling off the side. He sat up and crawled into the corner as Joe locked the door.

Vinnie lifted him by the shirt and slammed his fist into his greasy face, shattering his front teeth and breaking his nose in one blow. Blood gushed as Vinnie dropped him on the bed. Vito took out the zip ties and strapped his arms together, hooking them to the cheap metal headboard. Vinnie flicked open his switchblade and slit the man's pants from his body, boxers and all. Leaving his skinny body naked and twitching on the bed.

Joe sat down to watch as the brothers flayed the man's flesh from his body, peeled layers of skin from his leg, stomach, and arms. His entire body convulsed and shuddered with every cut; the screams muffled by the clown wig stuffed in his mouth. The red rubber nose had been shoved back onto his broken nose. The white greasepaint was smeared with blood and a ludicrous smile outlined his mouth.

When the boys had finished, Joe stood up, removed his suit jacket, and silently held out his hand for the blade. Vinnie handed it to him. Joe walked over to Weasel and cut his eyelids off, slapping him to keep him awake.

"I told you if I ever caught you trying to lay a hand on Maria, I would cut your balls off," Joe spoke directly to Weasel, right in his ear. Calm and cool, as the ruined man cried tears of blood, feebly shaking his head from side to side.

"You will not look away," Joe ordered him as Vito came around and shoved pillows under the clown's head as Joe made the first cut. Weasel's shrieks filled the room as Joe carved around the fleshy tip of his shaft, then slid the blade down the flaccid member. Blood spurted as each vein was sliced open by the knife. He sliced the scrotum open, cutting through the soft sac that protected his nuts. One by one, he popped them out and dropped them on Weasel's spasming body. By the time Joe finished peeling the skin from the man's limp penis, Weasel had died, with his eyes wide open, his testicles resting on his bloody chest.

The men stood quietly for a moment looking at the carnage, then began to clean up. They left and returned to their casino, gambling the rest of the night. Vinnie got on a hot streak at Blackjack and cashed in for five hundred large by the time they quit for the night. By noon the next day, they were on a flight back to the Bronx.

～

JOE STOOD QUIETLY IN THE BACKYARD OF THE BROWNSTONE HE AND ROXIE had shared for twenty-five years, watering her roses and talking to her softly. When he finished, he pulled the remaining packets of ashes from his pocket and carefully sprinkled them around each rose bush.

"You were a saint, Roxie, an absolute saint. The boys said thank you. Maria did too. She smiles more these days. She knows she is safe now, thanks to you." Joe kissed his fingertips and patted the dirt.

"Rest well, my love. I finished your list."

THE BEST PUPPET SHOW
IN TOWN

She stove the baby's head in with the cast-iron skillet; it burst
like a pale ripe melon.

Laughing at that moment was exactly the wrong thing to
do. As the shards scattered across the kitchen, my chuckle grew to a
full-blown belly laugh. Patty glared at me, madness in her eyes, as
she slammed the skillet down on the baby's head again. Black goo
splattered her body as she went to lift the skillet again.

I composed myself and lunged for her arm, pulling her away,
holding my broken wife as she sobbed. I shook with restrained
laughter as I held her, but soon her heartache unleashed my
hysterics and we collapsed to the floor, sobbing and spent. I don't
know where it all went wrong, or when.

I helped her to her feet when she cried out and took her to the
bed in the back of our old airstream. I re-bandaged her stitched and
stapled torso, then cleaned the blood from her thighs, the last
evidence of where the puppet child had tried to root once more.
Weeks of this had damn near killed Patty as our abomination tried to
complete its rebirth on its own. Days of our defiance to the Madam
had become our undoing.

Pulling the curtain closed across the minuscule bedroom, I began cleaning the shards of the baby doll up. Madam X had some explaining to do. I shuddered as I gathered the pieces up, the outside still gleaming porcelain while the inside was organic pulp and just beginning to turn pink. Rancid ichor oozed from the forming tissues and one eyelid still blinked at me when I picked it up and set it in the bowl with the others.

This was the third one that we had failed to complete. Patty was becoming more distraught each time, and I was rapidly running out of excuses. I finished picking up the pieces, then grabbed the mop to scrub the putrid slime from the faded floor. I grabbed my jacket and the bowl of shattered baby doll parts and left the camper. The sounds of the midway assaulted me as I wove my way between the old campers and RVs scattered about the backfield.

The carnival life was a hard one, money was tight, and the faded campers showed every dent and scratch, as did their owners. Many of the old carnies sat around the flames of dying fires, sharing stories and bottles. Drinking away their woes and drowning in a lifetime of regret. Some of them were passed out in the weeds; somewhere, someone wept, lost in their grief. Litter blew through the field like errant tumbleweeds, as forgotten as this wretched group of humanity.

I passed the back of the sideshow tent and nodded at the lobster boy as he stood outside, eating a corn dog slathered in mustard, his bi-pedal claws barely clasping the stick as he chewed the fried concoction. He reeked of alcohol and unwashed clothes, his hair greasy and plastered to his cheeks.

"Where in the hell did YOU come from?" I heard him sneer as I passed by. "You look like shit," he spat as I ignored him. He had always been a little shit, regardless of how kind I was. I sighed and continued my path around the freak tent.

Through the tent flap, I could see the fat man, *Tony Ten Tons*, and Leyla, *The World's Largest Bearded Lady*, taking tickets as they led the townies through the sideshow tent. Tiny Tonya hailed as *The Real*

Thumbelina stood on her tiny stage, her lacy gown fluttering in the stale breeze as the fake jewels of her tiara glittered under the fairy lights that graced her backdrop.

I shook my head as I saw how sallow her cheeks were and how jaundiced her skin was under the lights and heavy make-up. Her liver had been failing her for months now. We all knew it was just a matter of time before she dropped dead, maybe even on stage. I looked down the midway, past The Whip and its raucous music, past The Carousel and its horses with their slightly evil toothy grins, to the black tent that stood in the middle of the grounds. Purple and blue lights flashed from within, and a steady stream of fog flowed from underneath due to the fog machine that was kept running at the back of the tent.

Across from the tent stood Patty's Puppet Parlor, the small wagon that Patty and I owned, once painted a bright red, but now faded to brick and dirty brown. Patty had been a puppeteer for almost twenty years now, starting when she was just fourteen and learning from her father. He traveled the Carnie circuit and raised Patty on the same. Her collection of puppets from around the world were the most valuable things we owned, but Patty was willing to give them all up for the one thing she considered priceless: a baby of her own.

I steeled myself for the confrontation as I hesitated outside of the tent flaps, the beaded curtains jangling as the breeze swirled through and dispersed.

"Enter, Markus," her voice called to me, all cigarettes and sandpaper in my ear. Frowning, I pushed aside the beads and walked inside the fog-filled space, lit by flashes of light. The scent of sandalwood and patchouli hung heavy in the air; a heady aroma that often left you dazed and disoriented if you inhaled it for too long. Of course, the mild psychedelic that she blended with it didn't help matters.

"Madam," I greeted her as I stepped inside, trying not to look at the shrunken heads on display behind her, nor the tiny head of a child that floated within her crystal ball. The pitch-black veil over her body did nothing to detract from her shapely figure or piercing hazel eyes. I knew nothing was under the veil but another layer of lace, a form-fitting catsuit worthy of any supermodel, but was instead sheathing a demon disguised as a siren. All smoke and mirrors, seduction and lust, people threw money down to hear their fortunes, as told by the dead child in the ball, as visions poured across their frontal cortex, thanks to the drug-laden fog machine.

"What is it, Markus? Come to return the child?" She purred, barely concealing the mirth in her voice.

"You know damn well why I am here," I spat angrily as I set the bowl in front of her. "Fix it. You made a promise!" My voice broke as I spoke, from fear or from anger,I knew not. "Patty can't take much more of this."

"Sit. Down." Madame spoke with a deadly calm, each word clipped, bitten off like one might bite the head off a snake.

I sat.

"Did you tell her what was needed?"

I hung my head in shame. "I could not. She can't bear it."

"She will bear it if she wishes the child to be whole. It cannot exist forever in its puppet state. You must complete the birth in full."

"But you did not tell us that it would take this, that it would cost this," I whispered brokenly.

"You came with a wish, a wish that you begged me to grant. You did not care for the price, nor did you ask of the how." Madame stared at me with eyes reminiscent of warm honey.

"Do you still wish it? The life of your child to be reinstated?"

"Yes." I hung my head in desperation and shame.

"Strip." She stood, and the veil slid off, revealing her seductive form, taut and sensual like a panther, covered in a thin layer of lace that clung to her nude body. Her caramel skin glowed in the light and her breasts strained the lace stretched over her with every move. The mist began to swirl around us as a heightened tribal drumbeat began to pulse in my veins. I removed my clothing as ordered, shame coloring my face.

She removed the parts of the baby doll from the bowl and laid them out on the table, putting it back together like one might assemble a puzzle. I watched, naked and awkward, in front of her. A normal man might have been rock hard and ready to mount a bale of hay at this point, but I was flaccid and sick to my core, watching her handle the flesh-filled pieces of glass. The black gore clung to her fingers as she re-created the baby doll, carefully closing the gaps the best she could. A twisted smile clung to the edges of her full lips as she manipulated the shattered parts.

Fear and loathing consumed me, and repulsed my very nature as she slid the lace down to her feet. A goddess in all her glory, beauty personified; her hair flowed in waves down her back as the silver chain shimmered on her skin as it ran from her nipple rings to the small hoop just in between, down to her belly button, and around her waist. I shuddered as I saw the fine line that ran from her womb up to her chest cavity. Nestled between her breasts was the silver zipper.

"Unzip me," she commanded as she faced me. My hands trembled as I began to pull the zipper, reminding myself to not move, as her skin peeled apart and blood began to flow in crimson sheets, painting her torso, legs, and feet in gore. The tentacles within her began to worm their way out. Thick, ropy strands of muscle and sinew began lifting the pieces of the broken puppet and inserting them inside her. I finished unzipping her silken flesh, all the way to her groin, and a smaller appendage slid from her pelvis to my limp member and began slithering around the shaft.

I groaned as I stood trapped in a pool of blood at my feet. A warped succubus bride in front of me, with a demon of unholy design, tucked inside her lithe body. The appendage stroking me increased its pace, and I groaned involuntarily as my cock responded on a physical level. I saw her through the haze of green mist, grinning at me, teeth bared like a jungle cat as she trembled from the machinations of the atrocity within her. Blood flowed from her, coated her thighs and mine as the things slithered between us, pleasuring us both as they performed whatever cursed deed she needed them to do to remake the doll, the broken remains of my baby Grace.

The mist rose higher, and shadows filled it. Devils and beasts lunged toward us and skittered away. The carnie freaks filed in with blank faces and glazed eyes. They fornicated on the ground, shrouded in the sickly fog, grunting like animals. The scent of sex and blood filled the air as they cavorted like fiends from Hell. The drums pounded in my ears, filling my skull with noise, then pain, as it became frantic and chaotic. I screamed as I convulsed with alien release as the madam shrieked maniacal laughter.

The madam trembled and writhed before me as the corded tentacles finished filling her bloody cavity with shards of porcelain flesh. When the appendages finally receded, my body was trembling, slick with blood, sweat, and tears. The doll parts were gone, buried within her womb, mingled with my guilt-ridden seed, writhing in a bloody amalgam of tissue, ashes from my dead child, and glass.

I collapsed, spent, on the ground, helpless to do anything more than watch as the madam zipped her skin closed and went over to the pile of velvet cushions in the back where she normally slept. Her abdomen was already beginning to swell as she arranged herself in a comfortable position. The carnie freaks came to me then, two of them lifting me from the ground, taking me to the back where I stood limply while they hosed me down like an animal, dressed me, then deposited me at the small table where the unholy conception had taken place.

I watched, sickened, but morbidly intrigued as the madam began to moan, ripples shuddering through her as her womb expanded tenfold. The mist had receded, and my mind was clearer than before. The worst of this night was almost over. The freaks and carnies vanished into the night, except for her handlers, and they almost blended in with the tent. Their features and clothing were so dark they were almost invisible inside the gloomy interior.

A chanting began, slow and guttural. Madam's skin undulated as the thing grew inside her. I could see the tentacles writhing just beneath the glistening skin of her stomach and her swollen breasts as they wove their way through her flesh. The drums began again, though there was no music playing in the tent; it was coming from her, her mind infiltrating mine as the child grew within, and her pain intensified. I could do nothing but wait until I was summoned. My body was no longer my own, my limbs would not move, and my brain would not command. I was hers until the child was born.

For an hour, I sat and waited as the carnival sounds began to fade around us, shutting down for the night. Smells of hay, manure, fair food, and body odor drifted through the gaps under the tent, mingling with the scent of sex and blood. The handlers lit a series of candles and placed them so we could see. Just as they finished, Madam's legs dropped open, exposing her smooth pelvis. Her thighs quivered as the tentacles began to slither out from the glistening folds of her sex, two and then four, wriggling forth and suctioning to her thighs on either side, pulling her open from the inside. I saw her hips shift and move apart as the mound of her belly began to contract beneath the building pressure.

Fluid began to spill from her as she continued to chant. The handlers went to her, one at her head, one at her feet, and waited. I saw her eyes roll back as the drums reverberated in my own. A terrible ripping filled the air like a long strand of Velcro being pulled from a fur coat, and the handler waiting at her head leaned over her and gripped her arms, holding her firmly as she writhed in pain. A small appendage appeared between her legs as the reformed puppet baby began to crawl forward. The other shadow at her feet gently lifted her thighs and held them further apart, allowing more room for the thing to re-enter the world.

I watched in horror as the puppet, remade in the exact visage of my daughter, came forth, dripping and glistening under red slime. Vile liquid spilled forth as the thing popped its head out of her like a cork coming off a wine bottle. A squall issued from its tiny frozen mouth as it twisted and tugged on the ropy appendages aiding its birth. Madam chanted. My puppet child squalled. I could only watch in horror as it finished and laid in the puddle of filth as the drums receded from my brain once more.

The waiting men began assisting the madam, cleaning her and the thing she had spawned. When she was settled and resting, sheathed in her lace gown, I was handed the small bundle that spelled my doom.

"Now, you know what to do," Madam said, her voice still calm and strong. "Take her home, tell your wife that we must finish the birth and the child will be whole. If you do not, your wife will pay the consequences."

"Yes, Madam." I rose, finding my strength and autonomy had been returned to me once more. "I understand." I held the puppet to my chest. Not quite like a baby, more like a dead animal that you did not want to be close to your person. The horror clutching at my coat cooed, and I felt faint as I left the midway and the madam behind, taking the replica of my daughter back to my wife.

When I entered the camper, shell-shocked and weak-kneed, I was drained on every level. I could feel the thing sucking my essence from me as its small hands clutched my coat with surprising strength. Patty rose from the bed and took it from me, her eyes almost as sunken as mine own. Months of sleepless nights and grieving had taken its toll on both of us and then Madams' gift had gone wrong.

"Must it be now?" Patty whispered to me, cradling the puppet to her breast, marveling at its perfect features. It could be our daughter, alive once more, if it were not for the cold enamel of its skin.

"Not immediately, but soon," I responded. "I need to rest first. I need time." I met her eyes with mine, shame, fear, and bitter acceptance reflected in our gaze.

She nodded, and I moved to the bed while she took the child to the small table near the camper door. I collapsed and fell into a deep sleep, the cooing puppet the last sound I heard.

W<small>HEN</small> I <small>FINALLY AWOKE FROM MY HELL-INFUSED SLUMBER, DAYLIGHT WAS</small> streaming through the cheap plastic blinds in the minuscule bedroom. Patty sat stiffly beside me, the baby on her lap, also sitting stiffly, its bright glass eyes staring at me quizzically. It cooed, and it sounded like shards of glass being ground into my ears. Two porcelain arms reached for me, and I recoiled automatically. It cooed again and again; the sounds of rupturing glass filling my eardrums once more.

I sat up, gingerly setting my feet on the floor, then picked the baby up by its strings, letting it dangle in the air, spinning and twirling its chubby arms and legs. It grinned from drooling lips between the dimpled plump cheeks that were forever rosy, red from painted-on rouge. The hair was downy soft, and fine, like corn silk, blacker than the night sky, and fell in short waves around the rounded enamel face.

I just stared at it, disgusted and heartbroken for this thing that our daughter had become. Some hideous perversion of child and puppet, borne first from the womb of my wife, dying tragically within weeks, then a second and third time by Madam X. Each abomination borne from the seductress had gone awry because we had been unable to fully complete the ritual. This time, we would finish it, or Patty would pay the ultimate price.

I lifted my puppet daughter and set it on the bed, upright against the pillows, and turned to my wife with an agonized look on my face. "It's time."

"Isn't there another way?" she asked quietly, her eyes glassy with unshed tears. I sighed and tilted her face up to mine.

"Do you not remember all those sleepless nights? Our daughter made of glass, forcing herself inside your womb, again and again, trying to find her way home? Do you not remember how she sliced you open with a ragged shard of glass? She must be made whole or the thing that she is will continue to seek its way to your womb, to complete the rebirth that it was promised. I cannot stitch you up again, nor can we take it back. We must finish what we promised to Grace." I kissed her lips gently as more tears filled her eyes.

One fell as she blinked, and it rolled down her cheek, dipped into the corner of thin lips, and dropped from her chin. Another tear followed suit even as she stood, gathered the child up, and followed me to the freak show tent. Madame would only wait for so long.

Outside, the carnival was still, far too early for many of the carnies to be awake, but those that were needed would be. I led the way around the dilapidated campers, RVs, and vans that huddled in the desolate field like a backwoods junkyard, rather than a traveling fair. The sour stench of alcohol-laced vomit and day-old fry grease and corn dogs filled the air. Feral cats roamed the grounds, lapping up whatever vestiges of food and filth remained.

I looked neither left nor right as I led Patty and the puppet baby to the tent, a sultry mist already roiling beneath its edges in the dead grass. I could feel the freaks behind us. All seven of them silently trailed us to the tent. They were here to see this through. I could sense their anger and determination as they followed, daggers of ice chilling my back from their cold, emotionless eyes.

I held the tent flaps open for Patty and the freaks and watched them file inside, my guts writhing like angry snakes as bile crept up the back of my throat, burning it slowly as the acid lingered there. I swallowed it down as I took a breath and followed my fate inside.

❧

MADAM X STOOD BEFORE US, A RAISED BED IN THE MIDDLE, A PILE OF blankets and cushions spread out in front of her. Naked, and glistening, she sensually moved her body in a misty shroud of green smoke as the silver chain shimmered against her skin. I felt the drumbeats before I heard them throbbing through the ground beneath our feet. The mist rose and pulsed with flashes of green as the carnie freaks formed a circle around her with the fat lady in front. Madam's handlers emerged from the shadows and helped Leyla, *The World's Largest Bearded Lady*, lie down, her massive bulk rippling as she reclined on the blankets.

They cut her housedress from her with a ceremonial sword as the drums began to swell. Madam's voluptuous breasts swung back and forth with the beat, her long hair cascading to her broad hips. I could see the tentacles rippling under her skin, long rope-like bulges on her sides, and wriggling down her inner thighs. Several began to slide out from her labia, curling around her legs. More of the worm-like horrors birthed from her nether regions and slid down to Leyla at her feet.

I retched, too horrified to turn away, as they began to slither into Leyla, squirming and squelching around her pale fleshy thighs, and disappearing inside of her mountainous bulk. Minutes passed as the creatures made their way inside her, and Leyla groaned and gasped. Her stomach was alive with movement, a dozen shapes bulging and shifting under her skin.

The freaks began to chant as Madam climbed off the pedestal. She came over to Patty and me and pointed to our clothing. We nodded and began to strip as the lobster boy took our puppet daughter from us, carrying her by her strings. The puppet baby twirled and dangled in his oversized claws, drooling as her head spun around and around. The mist rose and fell, flashes of green light scented with sex and alcohol.

Madam walked over to Leyla and ran her hands along her smooth flesh. Leyla was beautiful, just a mountain of perfect ivory flesh, and silken hair on her chin. She gazed adoringly at Madam with shimmering green eyes, as Madam found the zipper hidden between her pendulous breasts and began to unzip her hidden seam. Leyla let her legs drop open, her sex on display. Madam pulled the zipper slowly as blood began to pour. Sheets of crimson gore poured out onto the cushioned floor.

Her flesh parted. The handlers began to roll it down over her sides, like removing slabs of sod from a lawn. The mounds of tissue that had been her breasts flattened and slid off her body like hot butter. Blood, tissue, bile, and layers of yellow fat glistened under the layers of flesh that fell away as her zipper finally stopped. Organs slid out in a waterfall of blood, squelching as they landed in the pool of crimson gore. Her intestines followed; thick meaty sounds filled the tent as they splatted into the growing lake of viscera as the tentacles wriggled through her emptying torso. The scarlet flood around her grew, merging with the grass and fog, glowing black in the pulsing light, coating the stomping feet of the spell-bound carnies still chanting blasphemous words.

Madam pointed to the carved-out cavern inside Leyla, gesturing for Patty to come near. Patty was pale and trembling, her legs barely able to hold her upright as Tony *Ten Tons*, and Tiny Tonya, *the Real Thumbelina*, trotted to her side and helped her walk forward.

Patty began to scream as the handlers came toward her, the tentacles rising and prodding at the air from inside the mass that was Leyla. The handlers, twin shadows laced with muscles and scars, lifted my wife and set her inside Leyla's gaping chamber. The eager appendages slid over her like overdressed pasta salad, wet and moist, wrapping around her limbs, squeezing her, condensing her until she disappeared inside the waiting womb.

I swallowed hard as my wife's screams echoed from the chamber of roiling flesh, then faded to barely audible whimpers. Tears poured from my face as sweat ran down my spine and seeped into the crack of my ass. I could not stop the trembling as the handlers came for me, lifting me by my elbows. They carried me to my fate.

My vision went gray as they began to feed me into the blood-soaked womb that waited for me. A thunderous chanting pounded through the tent as Madam began to shriek and howl, a weird laughter that chilled my core as the tentacles grasped me and pulled me into the torso of gore. My ears filled with the sounds of grinding glass as my puppet daughter cooed. The carnies were in a frenzied roar, snarling, growling, and tearing at their clothes as the drug-laden fog filled their senses.

∽

As the tentacles dragged me deeper inside the thing that was Leyla, I could see my wife beneath me. She was curled into a tight ball and growing smaller. Her fair skin had taken on a strange luster and was glistening with blood and fluids. I felt my own bones shifting and grinding under my skin as the appendages squeezed and churned around my body, contracting, and condensing as the drums reverberated around us. I could still hear the frenzy of the freaks outside as Madam shrieked and howled the god-awful words that would bring forth our rebirth.

I don't know how it came to this. I only wanted baby Grace to live, to fix my devastated wife. Madam X promised us fame and fortune, and the best puppet show on Earth if we agreed to her gift. Let her bring Grace back to us, submit to the ritual of rebirth, and we would live in luxury and fame forever. She did not describe whatever fresh hell this was; she made no indication that this was the price for our daughters' life. *'A ritual of rebirth.'* What the hell was I to think of that description? A drunkard does not make for a wise man.

I shuddered as my blood ran cold, then began to slow, sludging through my veins. I should have listened to the carnies that tried to warn me about the madam. I should have emptied the bottles the day we had Grace. There was a lot I should have done, but now it was far too late.

Desperate men do desperate deeds when it is redemption they seek. I never meant to hurt my daughter, my darling baby Grace. I never meant to find myself in an alcoholic disgrace. I only wanted a bit of sleep and a moment's peace from her incessant colicky screams. I picked up her to soothe her, but instead shook her like a beast. I shook until she rattled, her small head rolling on her shoulders. I shook her until she ceased and then I went to sleep.

Movement above me pulled me from the awful memory. I saw the tiny body of Grace being nestled inside Leyla. I heard the squelching of tissue and the moist sounds as the inner cavity seethed with tentacles and gore. The puppet strings of her limbs had been cut, and her delicate head faced down, glass eyes peering at me. Innocence shone forth from her cherubic cheeks and her mouth was pursed as if she needed to suckle. The final piece for the rebirth was done. Grace would live again when this nightmare ritual ended.

I averted my eyes, full of guilt and shame, and waited for my fate. I began to shudder and moan as my appendages began to stiffen and grow hard. My eyeballs shrunk within their sockets and froze like diamonds on the bone. My flesh was pale, a shell-like coating had formed on my fingers, hands, and arms. I knew if I could see them, my legs, my cock, and my feet would be covered in the same.

The contractions began to roll as the groping tentacles drug us down through her uterus and through the tunnel below. Everything went dark as the frenzied shrieks increased.

∾

WHEN IT WAS OVER, I BLINKED SLOWLY, UNABLE TO MOVE BUT NOT ABLE TO feel any pain. I could see bright lights and faces looming over me as I swam back to consciousness. I faded from gray to black and back again as I struggled to move, to stand, to comprehend where I was before I finally thought to scream. Sounds of broken glass filled the air as I did so, and I immediately stopped, confused.

I faded once more, passing from consciousness to nothingness. I existed in a vacuum, an abyss of silence. I knew no hunger, no pain, only the constant sound of glass every time I tried to scream. I did not know where Patty was or where my daughter was. I did not hear the mid-way or Madams' shrieking laugh. I just existed in this space until finally there was light, a light so bright but I could not look away.

∾

Faces and shapes loomed over me, and I felt myself being lifted and carried. I dangled in the hazy air, and I opened my eyes once more. Strings were laced through my hands, my feet, and through two places in my head. My body was hard and glazed, no longer the soft pale flesh that I knew. Someone spoke above me, and it sounded so far away that I could not make out the words. I tilted my head back, but it only flopped, and then I began to stare at the giant that was peering at me, both horrified and confused. The high-pitched voice grated in my ears.

"Daddy, it's time for you and Mommy to play! Madam painted the stage and everything!" My daughter, Grace, a girl once more, grown to a child of seven or eight, was speaking to me. Holding handfuls of strings, she dangled me and my wife from our cords and our boards over our old puppet stage, just inches from our storage trunk.

My wife dangled limply in our daughter's grasp. Her eyes were cold and staring, her face a mask of paint and porcelain. Her garments were fine and daintily stitched, and our stage was new and luxurious, filled with small furnishings of oak and gold.

Gold curtains hung in front, separating us from the stage. The lights dimmed, and the music began. My arms and legs began to dance as my wife spun around and around. Through the midway noise, I heard the barker begin to call.

My shimmering eyes could only widen as I suddenly arrived in my new reality. Madam had indeed kept her wish; I began to laugh hysterically, but only shattered glass ground within my painted-on ears.

"Come one! Come All! To the best puppet show in town!"

All around me echoed the madams' cackling laugh, cigarettes, and sandpaper, raspy whispers in my ears made of glass.

IN THE GARDEN

Irina rammed the shovel into the soft tissue of the body at her feet, neatly severing the head from the body with a final blow. Blood sprayed in a final gush as the jugular let go and the head lolled to the side, giving up its tenuous hold on the stringy bits of tendon it had been clinging to. She kicked it with a smirk, relishing the meaty sound that issued as her dainty foot connected with the caved in skull. The blank eyes stared at her, then at the dirt, then at the fence, and finally back to her smirking face as it rolled several feet, spinning to a slow stop in the freshly tilled soil.

She chuckled and dropped the shovel beside her. She stooped down, grabbed her water from the small wagon beside her and drank deeply of the tepid water. Her sweaty skin gleamed under the moonlight, drops of moisture glistening like diamonds as they rolled lazily down her neck, into her cleavage and disappeared. She put the water down, gripped her back, and arched slightly, twisting from her hips as she felt the knots loosen and relax. She sighed, ready to get this over with and get to her bed. It had been a long night, and she still needed to plant this body.

Irina shrugged, looking at the bloody soil beneath her feet, studying the corpse waiting for its impromptu burial. She took a couple of steps toward its feet, hovered over them, and bent to grab both legs, then she heaved the corpse backward to the waiting grave. It slid along, jostling slightly as the limbs bounced across the ground as she dragged it to the gaping hole in the earth. Irina glanced behind her as she went, making sure the body lined up with the length of the hole, then stopped. She released the legs with a heavy thud on the ground, then stepping to the side, Irina dropped to her knees in front of the crimson coated meat suit, bent forward, and gave a mighty shove, rolling what was left of her blind date into the ground.

That done, she sat back on her haunches with another deep sigh, exhaling fully as she looked around the dark yard. Pride filled her as her gaze roamed over the peonies and roses, the bluebells and hyacinths, the neatly trimmed hedges that lined her back fence, and the elegant water features that graced each corner. It truly was her private oasis, a little piece of heaven just for her. The gazebo on the far left was strung with solar lights that gave a warm glow, creating a delightful space to entertain guests.

The patio sat just behind it, connected to the gazebo and the house by a hand-placed river rock pathway. An impressive grill took up the far corner of the patio, hovering squat and gleaming under its bamboo shelter. Shelves stood beside it, with ample space for grill tools, propane, spices, and more. She liked things to be neat and orderly, both for efficiency and aesthetic.

She nodded absently as she rose and trudged over to retrieve the head, which was still staring at her with a cloudy gaze. The features were frozen in the last vestiges of a horrified scream, the mouth parted in shock. She bent over and gripped it by the shaggy blond hair, what was left of a poorly grown mohawk, and walked the few paces to the hole. She lifted it eye-level and stared at it once more, her lips curling into a smirk again, then dropped it into the hole.

She blew a droplet of sweat from the tip of her nose as she turned around once more to grab her shovel and the bag of lime. She had work to finish, dawn would be approaching soon, and her bed was calling her name. She wiped her hands on pants so saturated with blood and soil that she could only grimace when they came away bloodier than before. She wiped tendrils of her wavy brown hair away from her sweaty face, tossed her tools into the wagon, yanked it to the graveside, and got to work; her amber eyes turning dark as she lifted the lime and began to dump it over the body.

~

AN HOUR LATER, IRINA WEARILY STRIPPED HER CLOTHES OFF IN HER BASEMENT bathroom, added them to the pile of clothes she had cut from the meat suit currently fertilizing her garden, and dropped the whole bundle into a paper bag nearby. She walked nude to the shower and stepped inside, sighing blissfully as hot water began to stream over her body, rinsing dirt and blood from her flesh. Dark bruises stood out on her thighs, another one just beneath her rib cage, and a shadowy set of fingerprints wrapped around her upper arm. This one had put up quite a fight. He had no intention of tonight being his last night on Earth, but then again, Irina had not had intentions of fighting off yet another would-be rapist.

She sighed as tears filled her eyes, and she shuddered, remembering the feel of his clammy hands groping her breast, his tongue being forced into her mouth, and the panic that gripped her chest as he tried to unbutton her jeans. Irina had had enough of the abuse, the advances, the innuendos, and the flirting that were thinly veiled attempts at trying to bed her and add her to the notches on their bedpost. Three years ago, she finally fought back. She let the sobs come as the memories hit her, one after the other. Some wounds were decades old, some were still fresh, but all were scars opened and bled new, shattering her again as she stood sobbing beneath the water, letting it cleanse her, her soul, and her heart.

She stayed there until the water ran cold and her skin was bright red from the vicious scrubbing she had done, desperately trying to rid herself of even the memory of his hands on her. Irina stepped out, grabbed her towel, dried enough to not leave a water trail through her house, and wandered upstairs to her bedroom, leaving the kiln quietly humming in the dark, destroying all evidence of her night. She collapsed into her bed, body and mind aching from trauma, and fell into a deep sleep.

~

DELORES JONES STOOD IN HER BACKYARD, SMOKING WHILE SHE IDLY WATERED her flowerbeds, staring at the lush green lawn and flowerbeds that she adored so much. While her husband, Dirk, handled the lawn, the flowerbeds were her pride and joy. Dirk mowed the lawn and kept it trimmed, fed, and fertilized to her exact specifications. She fully intended to win their neighborhood Battle of the Backyards this summer. She squinted across the yard as she heard a door open nearby. Irina must have come outside to check on her yard.

Delores sneered and began moving slowly across the yard, dragging the snake-like garden hose behind her as she went, careful not to catch it on any of her prized plants. She walked up the slightly mounded side of her yard, closest to Irina's, and saw her just closing the lid on her grill. Jealousy seethed in her gut as she took in the sight of Irina's backyard, tropical in its beauty, greener than her own, and far more colorful with blooms of all kinds. She needed to get over there so she could see what all she was facing in the competition. There was still time to add some more variety to her flowerbeds before the contest next month.

She cursed as her forgotten cigarette burned her fingertips. She dropped it to the ground, flicked the water spray at it, then looked back over the fence. Irina was just barely visible at her grill.

"Hey neighbor, doing some grilling today?" Delores called out, shutting off the water spray as she did so. Irina spun around, looking startled as she did so. Delores watched her look around to see where the voice had come from, so she stuck her hand up in a brief wave.

"Over here, hun," she said, a bit louder than necessary.

"Oh hey, Delores. You startled me a little. How are you?" Irina said, stepping a few steps closer to the fence, but staying on her patio.

"Sorry, I just asked if you were grilling today?" Delores said with a tight smile. "Just out here watering the lawn and heard you come outside. When I saw you at the grill, I figured I'd ask. Dirk and I just got some wonderful T-bones. We could make a night of it." She grinned, watching discomfort crawl across Irina's face.

"Umm, that sounds great, but maybe another time. I was just adding fresh charcoal. Too much to do today," Irina replied with a tiny shrug of her shoulders offering a half apology. "Your yard looks great, by the way. I meant to tell you the other day."

"Thanks, isn't it wonderful?" Delores said, a hint of coldness in her voice. "I see you just planted a new flowerbed too. What kind?" she asked Irina, gesturing at the new flowerbed that graced Irina's backyard, just in front of the fence line. Rich dark soil gleamed beneath the late afternoon sun and rows of new greenery stood in their spots, just inches out of the ground.

"Oh, just a small variety. Nothing interesting," Irina replied dismissively. "I gotta get back to my chores and run some errands, but I hope you and Dirk have a great night with those steaks. We can plan a grill night later, maybe ask John and Edith to stop by." With that, Irina turned her back and walked back to the grill, pausing to open the grill lid before she disappeared inside.

Delores watched her go. Her eyes narrowed, and her pudgy lips twisted into a sneer. "Why that little bitch? How dare she?" She muttered as her neighbor disappeared. Delores knew she had been dismissed like a common stranger and she did not appreciate it, not one bit. She turned on her heel, marching back to the house. She and Dirk would be attending a cookout at Irina's that night, whether she liked it or not. No one turned Delores down, and she was not about to start accepting 'No' today.

❧

Irina stood at her patio door, just shy of the blinds, and watched Delores stalk across her yard, disappearing into her house. She could hear her shrill voice calling for her husband as the screen door slammed behind her. Irina chuckled before grabbing the bag of charcoal briquets from the floor and stepping outside with them. Delores would move mountains to get into Irina's backyard to see what the new plants were. She was desperate to win the ten-dollar trophy for Best Backyard from their neighborhood association garden party this year, but Irina found the whole thing trivial at best.

She had always been a natural green thumb. Her grandpa always said so. She never intended to win anything. She had been as shocked as everyone else when she had won last year. She just loved to plant things, all kinds of things, apparently. She smirked at her errant thought and finished with the grill, balling the empty bag up and tossing it into the trash can as she passed. She looked around her yard with a careful eye, pausing at the edge of the patio to do so. Everything looked as it should, not a pebble out of place, not a single weed invading the strategically placed beds.

Her eyes narrowed as she studied the new bed where last night's date lay rotting in pieces, looking for any telltale sign, any missed scrap of fabric, or a dark crimson stain on an emerald leaf. Something shimmered in the grass, catching her eye. She stepped off the path and walked over to the new plot of greenery. Bending down, she slid her fingers through the grass, searching for it. Her fingers brushed something hard, and she snagged it. When she brought her hand up, the zipper pull from the jacket of her date was held between her fingers. She stood, chuckling, and slid the tiny metal pull into her pocket, then brushed her hands off.

❧

ESTHER SAT IN FRONT OF HER WINDOW, STARING OUT OVER THE BACKYARD.
Dusk was just beginning to fall across the horizon as she watched
Irina dust her hands off as she rose from the lawn. She muttered to
herself as she continued watching Irina stroll back to her house.
From downstairs, she could hear Delores and Dirk screaming at each
other once more. They hated each other more than they had ever
loved each other. It was like they fed off each other's misery now. It
sustained them and gave them purpose. What purpose, Esther
would never know. Their marriage was nothing like the one she once
had with her husband, Harold.

Harold doted on her, and even more so on Delores until one day
he didn't. Why Harold changed, Esther claimed to not know. Why
Delores changed from sweet child to a sullen spiteful shrew, Esther
also claimed to not understand. Nothing made sense to her anymore,
even more so as time went by. Time made it easier to forget, easier to
deny and pretend. No one listened to her, anyway. They let her sit in
her room all day, alone, with nothing but the cats and the birds to
keep her company. Some days, Delores practically forgot she was
there, even forgetting to bring her meals until late in the evening.

Esther had been confined to this room since she broke her hip.
Only able to take small shuffling steps around the room before the
pain became unbearable. Her walker barely aided in her getting to
the toilet on time, let alone down the hallway or the staircase to the
kitchen. She continued rocking in the glider, absently watching Irina
disappear, then continued to sit there, staring at nothing until Petey
startled her by jumping into her lap.

"Goodness, Petey! You old shit. Going to give me a heart attack
one day," she scolded the old cat as he rolled his eyes at her and dug
his paws into the knitted blanket that covered her lap. He purred as
she began to stroke his back, her eyes finally focusing on the fur ball
rather than the window.

"You know, one of these days, someone is going to find out why
her garden is so green. You mark my word," she cackled as she spoke,
wry amusement sparkling in her eyes. "Maybe Delores will find out

soon. Her and that mangy husband of hers." Esther tittered to herself as she rocked. She was too damn old to meddle in other folks' business and, best she could tell, Irina was mightily justified in some of her recent plantings. She had no quarrel with her and, to be honest, Irina's backyard was more entertaining than anything on television these days. The girl had her grandpa's touch.

She heard Delores clomping up the stairs and smirked. *Must be feeding time,* she thought sourly to herself. *Wonder what it is tonight, more applesauce and mashed potatoes?* She was old, but for fuck's sake, not toothless or dead. A good steak would be nice, or hell, how about a nice roast chicken with all the sides and warm apple pie for dessert? She barely glanced over when the bedroom door opened, and her daughter walked in.

"Dinner, Ma. Sorry, it's late. Dirk was being an ass again. He forgot to get it ready," Delores grumbled, faking a smile as she set the tray on the wheeled table and brought it around to where Esther sat by the window.

"Oh? Did he forget to feed you too?" Esther said, eyeing her daughter, then the tray, barely repressing a sigh as she saw the applesauce cup with its plastic spoon.

"What? No, of course not. We plan on grilling with Irina tonight. He forgot to make yours."

Delores removed the lid from the plate and shuffled the plate toward her. A mound of mashed potatoes sat in the middle of it, with brown gravy and chunks of meat floating in it. Peas rimmed the soggy disposable tray and the ever-present applesauce cup sat there glaring at her like a leftover from a school lunch tray. She sighed as Delores stood there, waiting for her to heap praise on her.

"What's wrong now, Ma? You don't like pot roast?"

"Doesn't look like any pot roast I've ever made you," Esther said, turning her head from the repugnant mush and looking out the window again.

"Fine, don't eat it. What do I care?" Delores snapped, then stomped away. Her every movement was harsh and haughty, intended to make sure Esther, and anyone in earshot, knew she was ticked off.

Esther waited until her daughter slammed the door, then chuckled. Petey rolled a bored eye in her direction to see what the noise was, then butted his head against her wrinkled hand.

"She's so easy to rile up," she muttered, glancing at the steaming slop before her. Sighing, she reached for the cup of coffee that sat on the tray. At least Dirk made good coffee. The bread roll and day-old coffee cake next to it would have to be her supper tonight. She refused to touch anything else on that tray. It wouldn't kill them to bring her a decent meal sometimes.

She barely glanced over when Petey jumped on the tray and began sniffing at the meat stuff floating in the brown sludge. She chuckled when he made a gagging sound and turned away. Esther shifted her attention back to the window and sighed, almost content as night fell. The sky was clear; the stars were out, and at least she had coffee and cake, and a pretty garden as her view.

~

DELORES STOMPED DOWN THE STAIRS, SHRIEKING FOR DIRK AS SHE LUMBERED into the kitchen once more.

"That damn woman is going to be the death of me, Dirk. I swear to god. You better make her something else tomorrow. I'm sick of her bitching."

Dirk looked at her, unruffled. "You could always make her meals instead of sitting on your fat ass, you know," he sneered at her as she poked her head in the fridge again, grabbing yet another diet soda from it. "Those diet sodas are fooling no one," he added.

Delores gaped at him, then narrowed her eyes. "How dare you speak to me like that, you sniveling little bastard. You'd be nothing without me and you know it."

"Bitch, please. You do nothing all damn day long and expect to be rewarded for it. You leave your mother sitting in that room for days on end, unwashed and neglected. You expect me to work and wait on your fat ass all day and night and take care of your mother, and for what?" Dirk slammed the meat cleaver onto the steaks as he spoke. Each slap of the tool into the raw flesh made Delore's skin crawl.

"And for what?" He continued, "to keep up appearances for the goddamn neighborhood? To primp and preen over their dry sandwiches and weak punch during the yearly garden party and Christmas social? Those people despise you and you know it. You are nothing except a bitch that happens to hold a tiny modicum of power as Head of the Neighborhood Association. It's all you got, and that is all you live for. You're pathetic."

Dirk slammed the meat, again and again, punctuating his words. Bits of pink flesh flew and stuck to the tile backsplash. Delores stomped over to him and poked him in the chest with her plump finger.

"You listen to me, little man. I own this neighborhood and those people will best do what I say. I don't give a flying fuck what they think about me if they do what they're told, just like you better do. I can and I will make their life a living hell, as you already know." She backed away as he lifted the cleaver and stared at her, a dangerous look crossing his face as she stepped away.

"You don't have the balls," she spat, "now, take those steaks to Irina and tell her we will be there for dinner in thirty minutes. And please tell her not to overcook them."

She turned and stormed out of the kitchen, adding a final insult to her tirade. "And change your damn shirt. You look like a fucking circus clown."

Dirk watched her leave, snorted, and turned back to the steaks. "At least I'm not the one wearing the tent," he muttered. As her footsteps faded, he chuckled and went back to his food prep.

He set the steaks on a plate and sprinkled them with his seasoning blend. He knew good and goddamn well that Irina had said 'no' to the impromptu dinner party, and he didn't blame her. He had heard the entire conversation from the window, laughing at his shrew of a wife as she practically begged for an invitation. Everyone knew she wanted to get into Irina's backyard before the competition next week. It was killing her not being able to fully see it.

Technically, being the head of the H.O.A. disqualified her from competing, but she had created her loophole in years prior. She created a special "garden committee" to judge the competition, which allowed her to participate as she was not judging it, but since the committee reported to her, Delores still had a hand in the process. Everyone on it was hand-picked by Delores; those she thought were friendly enough to her and her way of doing things.

She had been quite surprised when the trophy last year went to Irina with only one vote for Delore's own backyard, of which Delores had cast herself. She had threatened to fire the entire committee as a result. Dirk chuckled, remembering the appalling shade of purple his wife's face had turned when she heard the vote, already half-risen from her seat, to accept what she thought was her trophy. His laughter had been the loudest as she stood there, humiliated, watching Irina cross the stage in front of her to take the trophy from Jackson Brown, the judge.

Dirk wiped the counters down, put his seasonings away, and began removing salad ingredients from the fridge. Once that was done, he lifted the plate and headed outside, stopping to flick on his grill before continuing to the gate that led to Irina's walkway. By the time she said no again, and they both had a chuckle, his grill would be hot enough for the meat.

～

DELORES STOOD FUMING IN HER BEDROOM AS SHE BROWSED HER CLOSET. So many clothes, so many colors. If there was one thing Delores loved more than her cakes and soda, and her garden, it was clothes. Her father used to reward her special behavior with pretty clothes. Delores never seemed to shake that habit. Whenever she deemed herself doing a good deed, she bought something pretty and new.

She never went anywhere fancy, had never been on a cruise or to a formal affair, yet she had enough clothes to wear to a year's worth of Broadway shows and black-tie affairs. She made excuses for it over and over as to why she wouldn't travel with Dirk, other than she hated him, of course. She couldn't stand the thought of someone in the neighborhood doing something without her verbal and written consent.

Why, the very thought of it pissed her off. Who knows what the Thompsons could get up to in ten days unsupervised? Or what about the Kinneys down the street? Those boneheads might paint their house purple while she was away. And those hipsters in the back? She shuddered, Beckett and Karlie Pastorelli, well, they just might start growing those marijuana plants in their backyard and put black patio furniture on their front porch. Delores might as well start allowing those colored folks to move in.

She can't allow that. It would be chaos, utter chaos, without her guidance and wisdom. She knew better than all of them did, and none of them dared to argue with her. She was responsible for keeping their property values up, the riffraff out, and the community spinning on a nicely balanced axle. An axle that she just happened to control.

Delores spied a silky leopard print shift dress that she loved and snagged it from the closet. It was trimmed in black satin around the hem and the sleeves, and the jersey fabric was comfortable without clinging to her rolls too much. She set it on the bed and selected her chunky black mules to go with it. She couldn't have Irina telling the neighbors that she had come to dinner in her gardening clothes. Satisfied, she trudged over to her dresser and began fumbling with make-up and hair products. She could hardly wait to see Irina's yard, finally.

∼

DIRK SIGHED AS HE APPROACHED IRINA'S FRONT DOOR. ALREADY RESIGNED TO doing what he was told, he shook his head and lifted his hand to knock. He knocked a polite three raps and waited. The steaks oozed light pink juices beneath the plastic wrap covering. He heard nothing from within the house and rapped again. Three more light knocks. Again, nothing, not a single sound emitted from within the dark house. Dirk grinned, pleased that Irina had not been home. At least they could avoid this little charade.

He almost skipped off the porch as he made his way back to his side of the fence. He was delighted at being able to piss in Delores' Wheaties once more. He trudged around his backyard and opened the grill, deftly added the steaks to it, and went inside. He would get the salad ready and throw some rolls in the oven to warm up. He made a mental note to save part of one steak for Esther's dinner the next day. He only served her the bullshit dinners that Delores insisted upon as she bought them frozen by the case, but even Petey wouldn't eat the stuff, most of which was liquid shit that a rat wouldn't piss on.

Esther had always been civil to him, despite the issues between him and Delores. He knew he was a shitty husband, but Delores was a shrew. Dirk never understood how Delores fell so far from the tree. He had loved her, once, but over time Delores' true nature had begun to show. She was a greedy, bitter, power-hungry woman who never had the motivation to do anything for herself. When her father disappeared, she had done everything she could to gain control over her mother's finances citing the tragedy and her mother's despair as incompetence. When Esther broke her hip, Delores had no choice but to take her in, secretly giddy that she now had full control over the paltry income her mother had from a modest pension and Social Security, as well what remained of her father's life's savings.

Dirk despised her for it, and for so many other things. At this point, he wished for her death daily, or for his own. It didn't matter. He truly only stayed to make sure someone fed Esther. The poor woman would be dead by now if he had left. Esther bore it all quietly, rarely choosing to speak her mind to either one. Dirk had realized long ago that whatever grudge Delores held against her, Esther chose to deal with it, rather than confront it.

He supposed no one would blame him if he left. But he secretly enjoyed making Delores miserable, too. It was the one joy in his very small life. He wasn't very attractive, and he knew it. He had an average job and was of average intelligence, overall, just a guy with a boring day job and a boring life. But he was now addicted to Delores' money, albeit ill-gotten, but nonetheless, he enjoyed his somewhat elevated lifestyle and the small bit of status it afforded him amongst his peers.

Porn was his main go-to for release, that, and nudie bars. Delores would shit her circus tents if she knew how much cash he spent on the strippers, but he didn't give a fuck. She hadn't touched him in years, and he doubted if he could even get his dick hard for her at this point. She had gained a lot of weight since their marriage and the odor that wafted off her lady parts was fetid and rancid, like old meat left to spoil. She had almost given up on her hygiene completely, choosing to douse herself in powders and perfumes until she smelled like a funeral parlor, death, decay, and makeup.

Her constant abuse of him and those around him had quickly killed whatever feelings he once had for her and all that was left now was loathing and the joy of one-upmanship that they frequently engaged in. He had mastered the art of pissing her off by simply not reacting to most of her insults. She was usually the first to fly into a fury at his lack of response, and that made him giddy with joy most times.

The sound of her pounding down the stairs pulled him from his thoughts and he fixed his face before she could see the amusement on his face. *Time for the next battle*, he thought wryly as he calmly added the salad dressing to the leafy greens and vegetables in the bowl. Her shadow fell across the doorway seconds before she entered the room.

"Why haven't you changed?" Delores demanded, sweeping into

the kitchen in a haze of hairspray and perfume. Her leopard print dress billowed around her, and the matching shawl draped over her shoulders like royalty.

"And what are you doing? Why are you still making food? Irina is probably waiting for us by now."

"No, my dear, she is not," Dirk said, not looking up from buttering the dinner rolls. "Irina is not home, and I know for a fact that she had told you 'no' in the first place. The steaks are on the grill on the patio and the wine is already poured. Go on out there like a good girl and sit down," he sneered, finally looking at her to see the color change on her face. He watched as the pink turned red, then crimson, then beet colored as she grew furious.

"What do you mean, not at home? I told her we would be over tonight. How dare she?" she began, her voice growing louder with every syllable.

"No, you practically commanded her to host dinner, and she very politely told you that she had things to do. I heard the entire conversation from the backdoor. Irina is not one of your little peons, nor will she ever be. She's not afraid of you like the other peasants on this block and, quite frankly, I'm sick of your tirades. Now go sit down or not, I don't give a damn what you do." With that said Dirk lifted the salad bowl and the basket of rolls and backed through the screen door to the patio.

Dirk hummed to himself as he went about making his plate. He sat down, laid a napkin neatly over his lap, and began to cut his steak, delighted with the slightly pink middle and the juices that oozed from it. He checked his watch, cast a glance at the door, and smiled to himself. Five minutes, Delores would storm through the door in exactly five minutes. Same routine, same rant. He'd heard it all before and, quite frankly, he was bored.

He began to eat and didn't bat an eye when Delores opened the patio door, let it slam behind her and yanked her chair out to sit down. Gone was the flowy dress and shawl, replaced with an oversized tunic and leggings that screamed for mercy as the threads held on to the seams along her thighs and ass. He almost snorted as she plopped into her chair and looked at him expectantly.

"Well?" she demanded.

"Well, what, dear?" he said, continuing to eat his dinner.

"Aren't you going to serve me?" she sneered, holding out her plate. "You know, do your job?"

"No, no, I am not. I am eating my dinner and I served it five minutes ago. Now, you can serve yourself. I'm not your housemaid." He pointed to the grill with his dripping steak knife. "It's waiting for you, right there, pink and bloody like you like it." He grinned with his mouth full at her and took a big swig of wine.

"How dare you speak to me like that? After all I've done for you? You get up, get up this instant, and make my plate!" Delores slapped the wine glass from his hand, sending it flying into the yard.

Dirk looked at her, smiled, then took her glass from her place setting and drank it down. Then calmly began to eat once more. After two more hearty bites, letting steak juice drip from his chin, he addressed his fuming wife.

"Delores, we have had this same talk many times. I do not mind cooking. But I will serve the food when it is done and when I am ready to eat. If you are late to the table, you can serve yourself like a normal adult. I've had enough of your petty tirades, your mother has had enough of you and your rants, and quite frankly, the entire neighborhood is just waiting for you to drop dead after one more late-night cheesecake binge. It would be a blessing to us all."

He watched, satisfied, as her jaw dropped open. Her eyes widened, then hardened, turning to glittering ebony stones in her eyes. Fury took hold and her face flushed. Dirk snorted and stood up before she could formulate another hateful tirade.

"Save it. I have nothing more to say to you and my dinner is done. I hope you enjoy yours."

Dirk picked up his empty plate, chugged the last drop of wine, smashed the glass onto the flagstone at her feet, and sauntered into the house.

❧

Esther chuckled as she backed slowly from the open window. "Well, I guess old Dirk has some balls after all, eh Petey?" she muttered to the old tomcat as he sat grooming himself on the bed. "Delores is going to pitch a fit just as soon as she finds her tongue again...but probably not until after she has her steak. The girl never did miss a meal."

She rolled over to the corner of the room and got settled with the T.V. remote. "Come on, Petey, time for our show. By the time it's over, it'll be time for the garden show." Her face twinkled with suppressed mirth. "Irina's garden show, that is." The big cat ambled over and got on her lap, an easy stretch from her bedside, and stretched out with a purr.

Esther clicked the remote on, winced as she heard the patio door slam, and turned the volume up a few more notches. Dirk was right on all accounts; she was sick of her daughter and her ways, regardless of the root cause. There was a time when every adult needed to confront their past and move beyond it. Esther had done all she could to right the wrongs and now, she was tired. Esther sighed as the theme song to her favorite show blared into the room just as Delores began shouting at Dirk downstairs.

❧

Irina walked up the short path from her driveway to her front door, ears perking up at the sound of shouting from next door. She paused for a moment, then shook her head. Sounded like Delores and Dirk were at it once more. Hopefully, they would quiet down before her headache became full-blown. She had a lot of work to do that night. She let herself inside, walked through the first floor without turning any lights on, and slipped outside to the patio. She took a moment to take in the fresh night air, grateful that she could not hear the bitter feuding out here.

Irina wandered around her yard, looking at the flowers and the many plants glowing brightly beneath the warm yellow solar lights that hung from her fence like magic candlesticks flickering along a wall. No bugs disturbed the many leaves and no signs of rot that she could detect. Nothing but the fresh scent of greenery, fragrant blooms, and rich soil. The backyard was the biggest in town, lush and beautiful, and truly her happy place. Her grandpa had taught her to plant her worries in the soil, deep down, where she didn't need to think about them ever again.

She smiled wistfully. Grandpa had her outside at two in the morning some nights, planting her nightmares way down deep where they couldn't hurt her anymore. She had found it silly at first, but realized as she drifted back to sleep that she felt better and that those dreams never came back. As an adult, she understood that it was simply the distraction that made her feel better, the cool soil on her skin, the night air whisking those bad thoughts away, not actually the nightmares being planted.

Grandpa used to give her lumps of coal to plant. Lumps of cold ebony sat heavy in her small hands while she described the nightmare to Grandpa, giving the coal the badness, then they would plant it together in the small holes she dug in the flowerbeds. When the bad thing was planted, Grandpa would plant a new flower over it; a pretty thing to cover up the bad thing. After that, and a glass of warm milk, Grandpa would send her back to bed with a full heart, a calm mind, and peaceful dreams. It was their thing. She never bothered to question why he was always in the garden so late at night, always digging and planting. She found out the night of her senior prom.

That was the first time she helped Grandpa plant something truly bad in the backyard, and she had been doing it ever since. There was no telling how many secrets were hidden beneath this expanse of land that she had inherited from Grandpa when he passed, how many years the soil had been fed with the blood of bad things, and the nightmares from her past. She did know that she was not the only person that had helped Grandpa plant his garden. There were a handful of residents still around that lived here when this land had been farms, others just trying to cope with the hand they were dealt. Now they lived quiet lives in the cul-de-sac, some in quaint carriage houses, some with their adult children. And all had welcomed her home with open arms and grateful memories.

She knew the depths of the soil held the carcass of her father, long thought missing, and the bodies of several young men that had not learned the meaning of 'no' until Grandpa and later, Irina herself, had taught them. How many others had also taught lessons of their own here, planted their own 'bad' here, she may never know. The earth kept those secrets hidden as it had been tilled and churned and mixed and burned over and over throughout the years. Her grandpa taught how to rotate small crops of vegetables and plot out flower beds for perfect blooms. How to properly fertilize and feed the earth so it would continue to take the bad things from her and provide for her.

Irina had to stop the practice when she moved to the city for college and, oh, the many bad things she had to endure. The city was no place for someone like her, no place at all. There was nowhere to plant the nightmares. No place to escape from roving eyes and groping hands. The constant threat around every corner, and perched on every bar stool, and gym franchise smoothie bar. She had grown weary of it all. Love, and all hope of it, had faded from her eyes long ago. When Grandpa died, she gladly moved back home and to the peace of their garden.

She had been dismayed to see that the over-developed neighborhood was now run by a mean-spirited bitch that could suck the fun out of a rave. It didn't help that Delores had been trying to buy the spacious plot of land from Irina's grandpa for years. It was the biggest property on the block, all that was left of the old farms that her grandpa and several others once owned. It bordered the deep woods behind the freshly developed cul-de-sac.

Still, Irina sought to make the best of it. She got along with her neighbors; she socialized when she could, and she kept up the garden, just like Grandpa had. And from time to time, when called upon, when necessary, she fed it the bad things, just like Grandpa had. Irina pulled herself from her reverie, hugged her arms close to her chest, and walked back to her dark house.

The shouting from next door intensified, and her heart crashed into her chest as something shattered and the resounding thud of heavy falling was heard. Someone shrieked then fell silent as the thudding stopped. Irina swiftly vanished inside her house as lights came on next door. She wanted nothing to do with whatever was going on with Delores and Dirk. It was bad enough that she lived beside the worst people on the block. Getting involved with any of their nonsense would be like signing her death warrant.

$\sim$

ESTHER SAT IN HER BED, THE PILLOWS BEHIND HER DOING NOTHING TO comfort her. Dirk and Delores had gotten into it badly that night, ending with Delores pushing the drunken Dirk down the stairs. Esther had been frozen in her chair, paralyzed in the sudden quiet of the aftermath, terrified for long minutes until she heard Dirk moaning in pain. She didn't know who had been hurt at first, or how badly. She couldn't get down the stairs on her own. She had no choice but to sit there and wait.

Delores's familiar footsteps clomped up the stairs soon after the moaning began, muttering cuss words as she passed by Esther's room. She didn't even stop when Esther called out to her. While Esther wasn't exactly relieved that Delores had not been hurt, she was glad that someone was still mobile. She had hobbled to her bed and lay down, turning on her shows to drown out the sounds of misery from below. She knew not to call for help. Delores very well might kill her for such a thing or put her in one of those vile care homes.

Esther shuddered at the thought. Nursing homes were simply tombs for the nearly dead, places for them to go to be forgotten.

Hidden away like shameful relics, far from polite society, where no one could see them drool on their bibs, or shit in their diapers like overgrown toddlers. Where people didn't have to see them and pity them or look away in disgust at their liver spots and white hairs, balding heads, and saggy breasts.

If it wasn't for Delores being so money hungry, Esther knew she would already be in such a place. Her room in Delores' house of horrors was small, but it was hers. A window to gaze out of, a bathroom of her own, and a cat purring in her ear. It was a luxury compared to any of those state homes. She wiped a lone tear from her eye and turned onto her side, tapping the lamp beside her to turn it off, resolving to begin a long night of trying to sleep and trying to forget.

Dirk's moans drifted to Esther's ears in the quiet night, and she sobbed, unable to help him or herself. He was an ass to most people, but he was good to her, as kind as he could be, despite Delore's constant harassment.

Her final waking thought was what would become of her if Dirk died?

~

BELOW ESTHER'S ROOM IN THE FOYER, DIRK SLOWLY BLED ON THE TILE floor; a puddle of vomit beneath him. He clutched warily at his head; bursts of bright light throbbed behind his closed lids. He felt the vein in his temple pulse with every breath he took. Pain skittered through him with every movement. His ankle screamed as he tried to adjust his position at the bottom of the steps. Delores had ended her tirade by smashing an antique vase over his head and shoving him from the top of the stairs. The wine Dirk consumed that night had not helped with his balance and he toppled, head over heels, backward down the staircase, crashing onto the tile floor with a violent shriek.

Vomit spewed from his gullet only a moment later, the red wine reeking of half-digested meat and stomach acid. Blood coated one side of his head and leaked into his eyes, rendering him half-blind with crimson rage and drunken indignation. He almost snickered, despite the pain he was in.This bitch really might kill him one day. Wonders may never cease. He was almost impressed by her attack. Then the pain hit, and his bemusement quickly gave way to guttural moans of pain.

His every attempt to stand made the room spin and his ankle was not cooperating with any type of movement. He gave up and lay there, blearily letting the room spin, watching spots dance before his eyes. Dirk vaguely saw his wife on the landing, sneering at him.

"I hope you're dead down there," she called out. "Rot in hell, you sniveling bastard."

She waited half a heartbeat before she turned and stomped off toward her room. Dirk had stopped calling it *their* room several years ago. The leopard print monstrosity of a room had ceased being his long before he set up residence in their guest room on the first floor. Mismatched animal print décor covered every surface. Shaggy rugs hid the old carpet and fluffy ottomans squatted in every corner, burdened with the weight of silken robes, moo-moos, and fuzzy slippers. The nightstand was covered in snack cake wrappers and half-empty diet soda bottles.

He snorted, picturing her laying in the giant four-poster bed, the dip in the middle threatening to swallow her whole. He could only wish. He grimaced in pain as he shifted once more, trying to find a position he could rest in. He would rest, and then he would get to his feet, somehow. Tomorrow, he would deal with Delores. Dirk retched as his hand slid into chunky vomit, trying to adjust to his side. The smell of blood, wine, and puke was thick in the air. He turned to the other side, trying to rid his nostrils of the cloying stench. Heaving a sigh, he closed his eyes and waited for the pain to lessen.

∾

ESTHER WOKE TO A SILENT HOUSE HOURS LATER, EARLY DAWN BEGINNING TO reach into her room with dainty pink fingers. The old cat grumbled, stretched his paws, stalked from the bed, giving the scant sunlight a haughty glare for having the audacity to wake him. She watched him leap to the floor, then rose herself, her bladder screaming for release. Esther struggled to sit upright, rolling her hips to the side before setting her legs over the edge and reaching for her walker.

Finally, on her wobbly feet, she grabbed hold of the walker, stretched her back as much as she could, then hobbled over to her bathroom. She stared at herself in the mirror for a long moment, seeking hints of the younger woman she used to be, then sighed at the futility of it. Esther hobbled to the toilet, hobbled the walker around in a half-circle, backing up to the cold porcelain before she was properly positioned enough to lower herself to the frigid seat.

She sighed wearily, letting nature run its course. Her stomach rolled within her, guts squirming like baby snakes filled her colon. Now that she was fully awake, the events of the night came back to her fully, and a slow dread had begun to fill her, a sensation she was far too familiar with, a feeling she finally learned to listen to, long ago, albeit too late. But right now, she was listening, hard. Dirk was an early riser, but she heard no sounds.

Delores usually slept late, but Dirk would normally be up by now, getting his coffee ready. He enjoyed the morning silence, relishing the few hours without Delores nagging at him. Esther finished her business, shakily rose from the commode, and shuffled to the sink once more to wash her hands. Petey twined between the legs of the walker, meowing impatiently. Another oddity for the day. Dirk would have fed him by now if he was awake.

She frowned at the cat, catching her gaze in the mirror once more. Glassy tears made her eyes shine in the warm light. Furrows marred her brow as she thought through what to do next. She did not want to wake Delores, not at any cost. That awful feeling in the pit of her stomach squirmed around to her spine and began to creep up her back, causing her to shudder. She grabbed onto the walker once more and started shuffling back to her room. She paused between her bed and the door, looking toward the door. The silence was consuming her. She sighed and headed to the door. She had to know.

Esther slowly pulled the bedroom door open and peered out into the shadowy hallway. Delores' door was still closed tight. Not a sound came from below, save the normal sounds of a functioning house. The ticking of the clocks, the faint hum, and whir of the refrigerator, and the odd glow of electronics as their panels displayed time and sat ready to power on. She shuffled into the hallway, willing the creaky walker to stay silent as she wheeled herself into the corridor. Esther reached the banister and peered over the edge. As she did so, her eyes grew wide and her bowels turned to liquid, soiling her freshly donned adult undergarments.

Dirk lay at the bottom of the staircase. Shards of glass littered the steps. A dark pool of something covered the floor beneath him and his eyes glinted in the low light. Eyes that were wide open and staring at nothing. The smell hit her soon after, wafting from below in a slow spiral of feces, clotting blood, and rancid wine. Delores stared in horror, transfixed.

Behind her, Delores's door suddenly crashed into the wall as she flung it open. Esther jumped, startled by the sudden noise, and whipped her head around to see her daughter staring at her, eyes narrowed.

"What are you doing out here? Get back in your room," Delores demanded.

"What have you done?" Esther whispered, hating the tremble in her voice. "Oh god, Delores, what have you done?"

Delores stomped over to her, rage contorting her face. "What the hell are you going on about, old woman? I've done nothing. I just got out here."

"Last night. I heard you screaming at him. I heard him fall."

"So what?" Delores sneered, "Not the first time he's fallen or been screamed at. He's a dumbass, and he deserved it."

Esther looked over the edge of the railing again, tears falling from her wrinkled face. She looked back at her daughter as Delores followed her gaze, realization finally hitting her as she saw Dirk's body in the foyer. Esther saw the blood leave her face, saw understanding, panic, then rage flash across her face in seconds. She was already turning the walker toward her room before Delores spoke again.

"Get in your room, old woman. I'll deal with you later." Delores pushed past her, and pounded down the hall, toward the back staircase, not toward Dirk's body.

～

ESTHER SHUFFLED AWAY, FEAR GRIPPING HER. DELORES WAS NOT GOING FOR help; she was going toward the basement. Panic consumed her old body as she entered her room, closed the door behind her, then leaned against it, shaking. Her mind raced with thoughts. She had no idea what to do or what her daughter would do.

A normal person would have called the police. Delores was far from normal, and she knew she had killed Dirk. What if Esther called the cops? What then? Delores would be arrested, sent to prison. Esther would be shipped off to a home, broke and destitute. The money would be eaten away by whatever lawyers Delores hired to save her, but there would be no saving her...or Esther, for that matter. So, what could she do? And how quickly could she do it?

Delores' pounding footsteps trembled through the house as she came back from the basement. Esther shuddered, fear gripping her. Her bladder let go once more, and she cursed herself and her age, disgusted by the scent of fear-soaked sweat and liquid shit that drifted from her body.

IRINA!

The thought came to her like a shout. A flashing neon sign. Irina would help. Esther had known her grandpa way back when the farms still thrived. Esther knew their secrets and in this moment was more grateful than ever that Irina had taken after her grandfather in more ways than one. As fast as she could, she hobbled over to the landline that Dirk had installed in the corner. She always kept the ringer for the phone silent, so Delores was unaware that she had a phone.

Dirk had argued with her for weeks over it, then finally hooked the phone up one afternoon while Delores was terrorizing the new couple down the block over the color of their patio furniture. He had told Esther that it was absurd that Delores treated her like a toddler and, god forbid, what if there was an emergency during the rare occasions that they left Esther alone?

She had thanked him and promised to keep it hidden. Esther had placed an empty hatbox over it with the lid removed and piled other boxes and books around it. Delores had never bothered glancing at the table in the corner, piled with the haphazard display. She barely stepped foot in the room, anyway.

Esther heard another crash from below and got moving toward the phone. Her walker wheeled before her crazily, crashing into the bedpost as she tried to navigate the narrow corner. She leaned forward when she reached the table, knocking the clutter into her rocking chair. Delores began cussing, her shrill voice reaching Esther's ears like nails on a chalkboard. Esther's gnarled fingers grabbed the phone and began to dial one of the three numbers taped to the underside of the box.

∾

Irina blinked in confusion as the persistent ringing of the phone woke her. She glanced around the room to find her phone, spied it on the nightstand, and grabbed it. She swiped the green call button and held it up to her ear.

"Irina?" a soft voice gasped out. "Irina, you gotta help me, please!"

"Who is this?" Irina asked, sitting up and swinging her legs off the bedside. The old voice was filled with fear, trembling as it spoke.

"Irina, it's me, Esther. From next door. Delores has gone crazy! She killed Dirk! Please, I'm scared. You gotta..."

"Wait, Esther. Slow down. Dirk is dead?" Irina found herself pulling on sweatpants and tugging a shirt over her head as she put Esther on speakerphone.

"Yes, yes, he's dead! She killed him. I'm so scared. I can't call the cops. Please, you gotta come. I hear her coming upstairs...Please, Irina, there's a key under the planter on the patio...Come...Aahh--"

Esther was cut off as a loud crash interrupted her words. Screaming followed, cursing, then a dial tone.

Irina quickly slid her feet into her shoes and bounded down the stairs two at a time to the basement. She spotted her pouch of tools, snagged it, then dashed up the stairs to the backdoor. She had no idea what was going on, but Esther couldn't defend herself and she had been a long-time family friend. Irina had to go. She owed it to her grandpa.

She burst through her backdoor, across the stone pathway to the gate between their houses and jogged around to the back. Two stone planters flanked their patio. Irina barely paused to decide before she bent and lifted the corner of the first one. Nothing. She darted across to the other and lifted the edge of it while she crouched down to see. She saw nothing, but stretched further, lifting the vase a bit higher, and reached again. There! Cold metal met her seeking fingers. She slid the key toward her, then snagged it, letting the planter back down as quietly as possible.

She could hear muffled shouting now, and a thud shook the window above her. That was Esther's room. Irina strode to the back-door, slid the key into the lock, and twisted it. It opened, and she slipped inside Delore's dark kitchen. The yelling was louder. A shriek met her ears and another thud. Irina reached inside her pouch, withdrew the razor-sharp blade she kept there, opened it, and then vanished into the corridor.

She barely glanced at the body in the foyer, only registering the state of Dirk's body at the foot of the stairs and the enormous pool of blood around his head. A flash of bone met her eyes as the gaping wound in his skull became more visible as she passed him to go upstairs. She shook her head and jogged up the treads on silent feet, blade ready in her hand.

~

"Stop, Delores! Stop!" Esther begged. "You don't have to do this." Esther cowered in the corner of her bedroom, her walker the only thing blocking Delore's attempts at slashing her. The room was in chaos. The nightstand overturned. Her lamp lay broken on its side. Delores raged, grabbing the walker, and tried to wrench it free from Esther's grasp again.

"I'm not going to jail for you," Delores shrieked. "Or for him! I'm not letting you take me down!"

"I won't say anything!" Esther cried out. "I swear!"

"It's too late for that. You already called someone. Now.. Tell. Me. Who." Delores screamed at her, punctuating her words with rapid thrusts of the kitchen knife she held.

Esther cowered deeper into the corner, shrinking back from her monstrous daughter. Then she caught the corner of the door moving, just the slightest motion, but it was enough. Hope burst free in her heart once more and she yelled at her daughter again, trying to hold her attention.

"He didn't deserve to die like that, Delores, no one does," Esther shrilled. "I don't even know who you are anymore." Esther shoved the walker at Delores, making her back up a step.

"I'm exactly what he made me!" Delores screamed back. "You knew, you knew all along and you did nothing!"

"You know nothing of what I've done for you!" Esther spat.. "You ungrateful cow! I've let you punish me for years but not anymore!"

Delores gasped as she felt a solid body behind her. She had no time at all to pivot around the edge of the bed to see who was there before she felt cold steel slip along her jowls like melted butter. Irina's blade sunk in deep, ripped through the tendon, cartilage, and thrumming veins before it slid out the other side, carving a new grin beneath Delore's spittle covered chin.

Blood sprayed across the room. Delores fell back with a wet gurgle and meaty thud on the floor. Her eyes rolled up to meet Irina's, who stood gazing down at her as the blood left her body. Esther could only watch as her daughter took her final breath. The mountain of flesh that had been Delores shuddered out a final rattling breath, then lay still.

Irina looked at Esther, offered her a kind smile, and stepped over the body to help Esther to her feet. Blood dripped from the four-poster bed, from the walls and the dresser, and from Irina's arms. Petey came out from under the bed, sniffed at the blood covering Delores, then pissed on her slipper-covered foot. He meowed indignantly as he left the room, still searching for his breakfast.

"I guess Petey didn't like her any more than I did," Irina chuckled as she led Esther from the room.

"Not many people did," Esther sighed in a defeated voice as Irina helped her into the main bathroom down the hall.

"I'm going to help you get cleaned up while you tell me what happened. Then I'll deal with the mess, okay?" Irina said to her, starting the shower.

Esther sniffed as she began to undress, allowing Irina to help. Tears flooded her eyes as she told her what had happened the night before and then the rest of it: Harolds' betrayal, Delores' childhood abuse, her own blindness. All the bad came out while Irina patiently listened.

"What are you going to do with them?" Esther asked. "I know what your grandpa used to do with the bad things," Esther said, watching Irina's face. "I know he taught you, too, just like he taught me." She finished in a whisper, holding Irina's gaze.

"Harold?" Irina finally asked.

"Beneath the petunias," came the simple reply.

~

6 WEEKS LATER.

Esther and Irina sat on the patio, looking over Irina's garden. It was in full bloom, and another blue ribbon hung from Irina's fridge for the Best Garden award. The cheap plastic trophy sat on the mantle in the dining room with the first. The vote was uncontested with Dirk and Delores still on their extended vacation. The neighborhood luncheon and garden tour had been a delightful afternoon and now Esther and Irina sat and watched twilight descend.

"Sure does look pretty," Esther said.

"It does. The new fertilizer helped the pansies bloom," Irina replied, grinning at her.

"That's fitting," Esther chuckled. "They were both pansies, anyway."

ALL IN DUE TIME

S terling groaned as the knife sank into the tender flesh that trembled beneath him, slicing through body fat, tissue, and muscle as smooth and easy as peanut butter, the gleaming blade crimson, and buried to the hilt. He did not hear the dwindling cries of his victim as they died, nor did he see the last bit of life fade from their eyes as their soul faded away into the ether.

He was lost in his bliss, finally breathing in this moment, after months of slowly suffocating on normality. He felt the power surge through his body as the blood poured over his hands. The knife flashed silver as it slashed deep into the cooling body, the rage fully controlling his every move as he shuddered with every cut. Time stood still as the knife arced over the corpse, again and again, releasing the only air that he needed to breathe. Deep, primal rage consumed him.

Time became inconsequential; it could have been hours or only minutes before he could do no more. He opened his eyes; a final profound shudder shook him to his core as his vision cleared. His right arm trembled with exhaustion as the blade clattered to the dirty floor. The body before him was no longer recognizable, not as male or female, young or old. It simply was a pile of bloody gore, ruined flesh and bone, cooling on a filthy floor.

He looked at his masterpiece splayed out before him, beautiful in its ravaged glory. His chest swelled once more with exhilaration. He picked up his blade, stood up, blood dripping from his nude body, and began to clean.

CHAPTER ONE

The knock at the door drew Grant from his study, where he had been checking his email and watching the stock market numbers. His investments were doing well, as they should be. He was meticulous in his trades and transactions. He was a partner at his investment firm for a reason. Being born into money of some note, his father had spent a lifetime grooming him to be successful at everything.

He could hear his father telling him, "All in due time," always telling Grant to slow down, to be patient, to know when the time was right before making a trade. Grant was watching the market before he was watching cartoons. Under his father's careful eye, Grant had amassed nearly $350,000 of his own money before he was sixteen.

He was a shoo-in for partner at Brandt, Brantley, & Bennett, one of the most lucrative investment firms on the East Coast, before he was twenty-six years old. The youngest partner ever. He had made them a fortune ever since, and they were paying him a king's ransom to do so.

He grinned as he closed his laptop and went to open the door. A third knock sounded by the time he reached the foyer, but he did not quicken his calm and measured steps. A walk that he honed to perfection over the years; one that he knew portrayed wealth, exuded confidence, and commanded attention. He opened the door with a practiced, gracious smile on his face, which he directed at the delivery person who stood on the threshold.

"Right on time! Come in, young man. You can set the bag down right there."

Grant spoke as if addressing a boardroom, all eye contact, and perfectly whitened teeth, as the young man stepped inside. He took his wallet out as the delivery person set the bag on the table in the foyer.

"This is a beautiful house, sir." The delivery driver stood looking around at the marble floor and polished mahogany staircase that curved up to the second floor. Elegant paintings led the way up the wide staircase and lined the upper hall. The foyer itself opened onto the library, the formal living room, and the dining room.

"Thank you. If you keep working hard and put in the time, you can have a place just like it, " Grant responded in a jovial tone as he held out two twenties, adding, "No change."

"Oh, I doubt that sir. I'm struggling in school now. Thank you for the tip, though. It's appreciated." The driver gave Grant a sheepish grin with a small, embarrassed shrug.

"Then allow me to offer one more tip. Good things come to those who wait. My father used to tell me, 'All in due time.' You need to wait for precisely the right moments in life to make the best moves. Not all success comes from a textbook." Grant offered the young man a handshake and opened the front door.

"Thank you, sir. I guess that makes sense. Is that how you got this house? Making the right moves?" The young man looked around once more, this time at the lush lawn that stretched out before him, at the wide front steps and curved driveway before looking back at Grant.

"But, of course, my friend. The right moves, at the right time." Grant gave him a wave as he turned to walk away. He watched him as he got in his car and then shut the door.

As he carried the bag of Thai food back to his study, he tried to dismiss the nagging feeling in his gut. Grant chalked it up to hunger and a bit of jealousy at the young man's youth and health. So much living left to do. Grant despised the aging process, and he detested the elderly most of all. The age spots, the shriveled skin, the hunched over posture, and shrinking of stature as life sucked them of their vitality, little by little.

The sheer audacity of nature being able to drain the health from its oldest and wisest seemed most unfair. Grant was of the mindset that the aged should be among the wealthiest, the most beautiful, the most revered people on earth. They are the ones who taught, raised generations, and built this world to be what it was. They are the ones that should be gifted, granted adoration, and long lives. Not left to shrivel and die in the sickening filth of nursing homes and hospitals, suffocating on the smell of their urine and shit.

He had to watch his father age, and he hated it. He was thankful when the old man passed of a violent heart attack when he hit seventy-five. Not a moment too soon, in his opinion. Grant loved his father. Make no mistake about that, he was his prodigy, his perfectly groomed clone. Grant worshipped the air his father breathed, as much as he hated it. But as the gray came and smothered the black from his hair, as heavy years shrunk his father's tall stature inch by inch and as gravity sunk his cheeks and wrinkled his eyes, Grant struggled with his father's easy acceptance of old age.

The older man was movie-star-attractive, well-read, highly intelligent, and commanded a room like no other. Grant loved going to work with him back then, watching from the corners as his father ran board meetings, made deals, and signed contracts. He loved the looks of respect his father received from all around him and, by default, Grant himself was also privy to and acknowledged with.

Grant was an observant man, and he saw how society quietly put their elderly away in homes and hospitals to pass away alone and senile, as the world replaced them with younger versions, more attractive versions. They no longer commanded respect or boardrooms. No longer feared in hallways or workplaces, only pitied and soothed like children.

He could not fathom his father succumbing to such a fate circle of life be damned. It hardly seemed fair. Those who paid their dues should not be paying such a price simply because they were born. He would be respected, above all else, for as long as he breathed.

Grant finished his lunch and his silent musings in a foul temperament. His prior pleasant mood having been ruined by his ruminations of aging, his father, and the life cycle. Grant was fifty-five and in damn near perfect health, but he knew it was coming. He felt the days marching by, like an executioner tapping out the hours with his blade... he could feel the beginning of the end. Hour by hour, he knew was getting older. He knew that he, too, would fade away into the ether like a silent specter. He loathed the inevitability and fought it daily.

"Oh, hell," he muttered and stood up, gathering the remains of his lunch to dispose of in the kitchen. Frustrated now and filled with anger, he could do little but address it. He needed an outlet. He walked through his quiet house, in rigid control of his increasing resentment, disposed of his trash, and stepped out the side door to the patio overlooking the pool. Shedding his clothes as he went, he strode down the length and dove into the twelve-foot depths, loving the chill that struck him almost senseless as he sank to the bottom.

He kept the pool water cold on purpose. He loved the sudden shock as it hit his body, like a thousand needles piercing his flesh as he dove. By the time he reached the other end of the pool, the sensation would pass, and his brain would feel more alert than ever, firing on all pistons. All senses heightened, his whole body at attention, blood pumping through his veins. It was an addiction. He walked up the pool steps, back to the other end, dove in and did it again. And again, each dive perfect and precise, each underwater swim to the other side flawlessly timed.

Grant did everything with purpose and intent; he found the addiction of routine soothing. A schedule kept his mind focused. His habit was to run through stock numbers and contracts in his head as he exercised, did menial household tasks, or drove. The perfection of his regime allowed him to operate on an efficient autopilot, freeing his attention for important aspects like client interaction and associate tasks.

Leaving the pool, he retrieved his clothes and continued around the sidewalk to the rear door of his house, entering the first-floor game room. He walked through the massive chamber to the small archway at the back and stepped inside a modest laundry room, changed his clothes, and walked out with clean white socks in his hand, still in the plastic packaging, and into his exercise room.

Grant was proud of his house; this space was his pride and joy. This was a room for a man to be proud of, well-stocked with weights, jump ropes, a rowing machine, a boxed-in corridor for axe-throwing and knife practice, with several targets hanging at the other end. The floor was polished and padded, sound-proofed and wired with speakers, two televisions, and one computer that monitored the stock ticker 24/7. The gym ran the length of the house, including the four-car garage at the end, giving Grant plenty of space for the exercise machines, a target practice arena, and sprinting track precisely a quarter mile long. At the far end, next to the door that led into the garage, resided a sauna and a private shower room.

He entered and sat down on the bench to his left, pulled on socks and shoes. He hit a few buttons on the remote control that stood nearby, and everything was flooded with blue strobe light and music while videos began to roll across the television screen. The rest of the house went into lockdown mode, as Grant allowed nothing to interrupt his workout. Soft lights emanated from the living room, kitchen, bedroom, front door, and garage as automatic door locks engaged.

The typical "suburban family not at home" starter security kit set-up. All pretenses, a show for his neighbors, should anyone come calling. Routines made everyone feel safe. Dark houses made people uncomfortable. If they could see the house, they would see warm, inviting light, safe and predictable light, for this time of late afternoon.

Grant stood on the exercise mat in front of the mirrored wall and began to stretch, music blaring, black and white video feeds still scrolling across the large T.V. screens. A sane person might not want to look too closely at the video feed that played across the large screens. He grinned at the mirror, loving his reflection. The well-muscled body moved like a machine, all broad shoulders and chiseled abs. He may be fifty-five on the books, but he had the physique of a man of thirty. Aging be damned. He grinned again before he began to work out in earnest, moving to his weight bench.

As Grant moved from machine to machine in his private inner sanctum, a lone car sat lingering on the street. Idling quietly across from the large, gated house, a form sat inside, staring out of the window. No headlights on, small nondescript car, just an outline of a person occupying the front seat. Twilight gave way to full darkness, and the small car pulled away from the curb, vanishing into the night.

CHAPTER TWO

Sterling stood in the dim light of the barn, using his knife to trace the curves of the body hanging there. The sharp blade cut smoothly into the flesh, leaving a fresh blood trail as the point reflected pale tissue in the moonlight. The body trembled and shook as it hung upside down from the overhead beams. A single hole in the old roof allowed the moonlight to shine right on their terrified features as they squirmed against their bonds, exactly as Sterling staged it. So enthralled was he by the scene he had set, he scarcely heard the panicked whimpers coming from his prey.

The naked flesh was pulled taut against the ropes that wrapped it, arms and legs lashed tight to the body. The ankles were bound and secured to the beam above by a giant hook that had been run through the heavy rope. The arms were strapped around the stomach and secured at the wrists in the back. The hair just barely grazed the dirt floor, a scant inch away from the face. They would smell mold and filth with every breath against their gag.

Sterling squatted as he continued tracing the blade down the arms, across the chest, around each puckered nipple, and back up to the jaw. When the prey squirmed against the blade, his massive fist shot out and grabbed hold of their hair, holding the head still as he pushed the blade just a bit deeper, watching the blood surface faster than before. He licked his lips, intensely focused on his task as muffled screams rent the air around him. Nobody would ever hear their cries, and it sounded like background music for the symphony that Sterling was conducting.

Tears poured from their eyes and ran down into their hairline, mingling with the blood dripping there, as the blade continued its exploration. Fear glistened in wide eyes as they locked with Sterling's, seeing nothing recognizable staring back, only emptiness. Not a shred of recognition, not a flare of emotion, no reaction whatsoever, just blackness. It was then, despite their obvious pain, that they began to hyperventilate, convulsing with intense fear.

Sterling was solely focused on his singular task, lost in the immense pleasure of the blood that now poured freely down the shaking body. Each path around the body, he dug deeper, watching more blood escape and race down the pale skin, red glowing black in the moonlight. The puddle around Sterling's feet grew wider as he began to peel long strips of skin from the legs, silently working the blade under the epidermis, as he extracted layer after layer free from each limb. The raw tissue and muscle underneath glistened scarlet as he exposed it. The guttural screams coming from his victim went unnoticed even as the body shuddered and jerked at his touch.

When he finished with the legs, he moved on to the thighs, and then the buttocks, peeling mounds of skin from each section, letting it drop to the bloody pool he stood in. The body hung still now except for the tugging motion Sterling made as he peeled the flesh from it. The person had passed out a long while ago, probably for the best, as he was nowhere near done. Blood covered him, almost as completely as the half-dead person he was mutilating. He worked in silence. His breath came in short grunts as he twisted and turned the body into a necessary position.

When the body was free of flesh, face, and scalp, he cut it down and watched it drop into the pile of bloody skin and tissue on the floor. The vertical gash he had made in its torso split open as it hit the filthy floor. Organs and loops of intestines spilled from the opening, jolting the unconscious victim awake. The eyes opened in the bloody skull that stared back at him, wide with fright and panic. The gag and the tongue were both gone, nothing but gurgling sounds issued forth as it tried to scream.

He stared at it for a long moment, apathetically, almost curiously as if he had never seen it before, then he raised the knife over his head and brought it down with a violent bellow of rage, a shudder racked his muscular frame as all his tension released and he exhaled freely, excitedly, alert, and awake. The time had come for him to become free, to breathe as he was meant to breathe, to be the God he was meant to become.

His arm raised again and again, stabbing, and ripping through the flesh beneath him as he breathed, in and out, slow, and deep, the anticipation more addicting than any drug he's ever had, as he squatted and stabbed, again and again, before finally drawing the blade across the throat of the eviscerated body and watching the remaining river of red rush out.

He bathed his hands in it and rubbed them across his face, down his chest, a final roar of pleasure, and victory, ripped from his chest, echoing around him in the empty barn. He stood in the middle of the moonlight, a pile of gore at his feet, blood dripping from his body as he breathed deeply, a savage grin dripping blood from his lips. He stood like that for long minutes, savoring another successful hunt. The exhilaration coursed through his body, the culmination of months of work at his feet.

When he was full, his chest and lungs expanded with tainted air. He flexed his muscled body, tendons, and joints popping as he did so before exhaling. He bent down and gathered the ruined body beneath him into his arms. Lifting the dripping mass to his chest, he walked it to the far corner of the barn and dropped it into the waiting pit. He made three more trips, collecting strips of flesh, bits of bone, scalp, and hair, and took those to the pit as well.

He began to clean the rest of the site, soaking up the blood, hosing down the site from the old water hose that he kept there, burying the rags, the rope, and the bits of clothes, deep in the hole he had dug. Once done, he shoveled in two feet of dirt and manure on top of the ruined body parts and viscera, then he dragged the rotting hog carcass over to the pit that he had killed a week earlier and shoved it in. He filled the rest of the hole in just as the sky was beginning to lighten with the first streaks of pink and orange.

～

GRANT ARRIVED HOME FROM ANOTHER BOARDROOM MEETING LATER THAT week, high on yet another victory. The firm's investments were performing better than ever, and it was from his recommendations. Everyone knew that he had made the firm more money than all the other partners combined. Grant was nothing short of a rock star as far as they were concerned. He was looking forward to a few days off this week and he had a short trip planned to the mountains in a couple of months. Just in time for the first snow, his father used to take him every winter; Grant continued the tradition.

A warm lodge, some century old Brandy, and archery would get the blood pumping like it hadn't been in a long time. Some hobbies he had less and less time for as he grew older and work grew more demanding, as much as he hated it. But he was nothing if not a patient man. His father had taught him well, and he found other hobbies that could help curb his appetite for that extreme adrenaline rush that hunting brought him. There was nothing quite like man versus prey in the wild, in the cold, in the worst of conditions. Grant enjoyed testing his limits. Once thoroughly trained, of course. Adrenaline junkie, perhaps, but stupid, never.

As he walked through his house to his study, he called the Thai place on his cell, placing his usual order. Sitting down at his desk, he put his briefcase down next to him and powered up the laptop to check the market and his email. By the time he had finished responding to some emails, making a few quick personal trades, and swapping his business clothes for casual clothes, the doorbell was ringing. His dinner was right on time. He loved punctuality, especially from a service such as a restaurant, and stayed loyal when one prided themselves on this attribute.

He reached the door just as the bell rang for the third time, and he opened it with a smile. The same delivery driver was there, waiting patiently with his order.

"Hello, again, young man. Perfect timing!" Grant stepped back, opening the door wider and gesturing for the driver to enter.

"Oh, hello again, sir. Nice to see you again." The driver set the food down on the small table in the foyer again, the exact spot as before. He looked around, admiring the staircase and the marble floors once more as Grant took out his wallet.

"This is such a beautiful place, sir. May I step into the living room? It's just such an amazing design." He looked hopefully at Grant as he took the money he held out.

"Of course, it's practically on display in front of you, anyway. Go right ahead."

Grant gestured to his left where the living room sat nestled just down two short marble stairs. Several couches situated on various levels all centered towards the massive fireplace in the back of the room. Black stone framed it, and exposed mahogany beams ran the length of the ceiling overhead. A baby grand sat in a corner of its own and built-in bookcases ran the length of the far wall while the wall facing the outside was all windows.

The young man stepped down into the sunken living room like one might step into a church, almost reverently, looking around with wide eyes. A low whistle came from his lips as he took it all in, leaving the exposed beams and bookcases for the longest inspection.

"This is really something. It's a nice eclectic blend of mid-century modern with modern contemporary design. It's incredible how well it all goes together." The delivery man was practically gushing as he looked around, rooted to his spot just at the bottom of the steps.

"Well, now, you do know your design, don't you? Is that the field you are in?" Grant stood at the top of the steps, trying to see the room from the eyes of the newcomer, appreciating his perspective. It was refreshing to speak to someone who recognized the design for what it was.

Grant walked down the steps, gesturing around the room as he spoke. "Many of these items belonged to my late parents and were pieces that I could not part with when they passed. When I built this place, I had the designers come up with an aesthetic that would honor both generations, my past, and my present. It's very important to honor where one comes from, don't you think?"

"Honestly, I've not thought about it like that before, sir, but yes, I do think it's important to know where we come from, to know why we do the things we do, to know our traditions and what they stand for, whatever those traditions might be."

"Well said," Grant replied, delight evident in his tone, "what is your name, young sir?"

"Oh, um, it's Braden, Braden Jones."

"Come in further. If you like, you may look around a bit. You don't need to hover at the steps." Grant gestured at the fireplace and the bookcases. "The stones for the fireplace were dug from the riverbed that ran through my grandmother's farm and those bookcases were hand-carved in Italy and assembled right here in the room. That wood can no longer be obtained here in the States." Grant gestured at various books and objects on the shelves, pride clear in his voice.

Braden followed him around the room, politely paying attention to every detail, the awe on his face growing more intense by the second. Grant had amassed an impressive library of rare books; volumes Braden had never heard of and some that were thought to only be rumors. He was equally impressed and intimidated by the wealth of knowledge on the shelves and coming from the man himself.

What seemed like an hour later but was only ten minutes or so, Grant concluded his mini-tour, and they were standing back in the foyer. Braden, still a bit awe-struck, suddenly remembered his job and where he was standing. He laughed a bit awkwardly before sticking out his hand to offer Grant a parting handshake.

"Thank you, sir, so much. This has been great. I'm a bit speechless. That's quite the collection you have there. I must go, but I appreciate you taking the time to show me. Maybe I will switch my major to design. It's a lot more interesting than heating and cooling skills."

Grant chuckled, "Well, heating and cooling is important too, and always needed, but one should always seek work in a field that excites them, something that they can find passion in. I wish you good luck in your studies, Braden." Grant ushered him out and carried his waiting dinner back to the kitchen.

He found his conversation with Braden to be both amusing and validating. Who doesn't like a little hero worship and adoration? He would bet his last dollar that when his order had been placed, Braden begged to deliver it. He was practically drooling over the house, probably the first time he had ever been in such a place. Grant didn't mind encouraging a bright mind to study; after all, they were the new generation. He certainly wasn't any competition for Grant in any capacity, so why not allow him to see what hard work and patience can do?

He grinned to himself again as he ate. Maybe he would order more Thai food over the weekend and give Braden another tour. Maybe the patio and pool area would blow his mind. He finished his meal and headed to the gym to work out for the evening.

As the lights to the house dimmed and switched to lockdown mode, a small car drove down the street and parked in the shadows across from the house. A lone figure sat in the dark, watching as the various lights rotated through their sequence, turning off most of the first floor's lights, then turning on various lamps, and then the outside porch and garage lights. Several hours passed before another light was turned on in an upstairs bedroom and the small car drove away.

CHAPTER THREE

Grant woke up with a startled gasp, clutching sweat-soaked sheets as his heart slammed against his chest. Waves of intense pleasure still trembled his limbs as he fought to regain control of his senses. Remnants of the dream fluttered through his mind, sheets of blood pouring down on him as a mighty roar of pleasure had ripped from his throat, a body at his feet, no more than a ruined pile of flesh.

Power washed over him, through him, setting him on fire from within, and his eyes glistened in the dark room. The beast in him would not be silenced, not this time. Grant thought he tamed it long ago, but it was awake and insistent once again. One more hunt called to him; the thrill of it, the anticipation of the kill, the power he held over the prey, and the power he would gain once the life was surrendered would be transcendent.

His breathing slowed, and the trembling stopped. Grant swung his legs off the bed and headed to the gym. Nothing else would do right now, not until he began the hunt. The beast would rage within him until then.

Minutes later, he stood tall and proud in front of his mirrored gym wall, clad only in sweatpants, staring at his chiseled chest, the veins rippling and bulging of their accord as he watched. His eyes flashed blue to grey, and back again;. Sterling, the beast within him, was fighting to gain control. Grant closed his eyes and submitted. When they opened, bright blue orbs stared back from the mirrored wall.

He roared at his reflection, sounding like a caged bear, before he slammed his hand into the wall, shattering part of the mirror. His canines glistened in the shards, looking longer and sharper than before. He grabbed the remote and jabbed at the buttons, setting the gym to workout mode.

Blue lights strobed and pulsed to angry metal as Sterling began to work the gym. The walls thumped with a beat of their own as the caged beast began throwing weights around like rag dolls. The veins in his body began to pop out as the muscles bulged from the heavy weights. Sterling relished the strength and power that coursed through his body.

Inside the mind of the beast, Grant watched and began to plan. The beast would have his hunt, but Grant would be at the helm. His meticulous planning had kept them safe this long, and it would continue to do so. No one knew his secret, and no one would ever catch him. He had what so many did not.

Patience.

~

IN THE MORNING, GRANT DRESSED AS NORMAL, WENT ABOUT HIS WORKDAY, and came home. His normal routine was on smooth autopilot all day as he studied people that he encountered along the way. Behind his dark glasses, one eye flashed roiling clouds of gray while the other stayed a piercing blue. The beast wanted to pick the prey. There was no hurry to this process, no need to rush.

The hunger had been acknowledged and accepted; nothing would stop it now. Sterling trusted Grant's process, he knew the final rewards would be his. They finished the evening routine and stepped into the gym. Changing into dark street clothes and a hat, they set the remote and the timer, then slipped out of the back door into the dimly lit yard.

The lawn was lush under his sneakered feet and Grant quietly walked the length of his backyard, to the hidden gate, and into the dark forest beyond. The wooded area stretched just over a mile and opened into a slightly poorer neighborhood than his own. Grant walked the streets as if he owned them. Just a nice older man, out for his evening stroll.

His keen eye observed everything as he ambled by the modest homes. Some had families at dinner, others had kids playing in the yard. Most had one car in their driveway, many older models, nothing fancy here. Simple lives lived with simple things. No security alarms, no cameras, and no police patrols. He saw a few dogs, several cats roamed the yards and perched in windows.

Grant nodded and smiled at those he passed. A wave to folks across the street, a polite word to a jogger and a teen on a bike. He liked it here. He had slipped right into character. In a week, the whole neighborhood would believe that he lived there, that he had been there forever.

He crossed the street and turned left, seeking the heart of the small community. They all had a Main Street somewhere, with the bar, the diner, the hairdresser, and the barber. A friendly church or two and a fire station. He could see it all in his head as he continued his steady pace through a town that wasn't his. He almost laughed aloud when Main Street showed itself, two streets over and looking like he had designed it himself.

A small park lay in the middle of the wide street. A gazebo stood proudly at its center, with a fountain perched in front. Small trees lined the street, interspersed between parking meters. There were two diners and a bakery, a small post office, and two small antique shops, along with the other obligatory establishments.

He wandered on, silently, observing all that he saw, that one blue eye always watching for its prey. Grant made mental notes while the beast's eye slid hungrily over every face, young and old, male, and female, every race, every background. It searched for a singular trait that only the beast understood. Grant would know when the target had been found and not a moment sooner.

He purposely stopped in the bakery, bought a coffee and a bear claw, then grabbed a newspaper from the small rack in the diner.

Waves and friendly greetings are all around. With a tip of his hat, he was gone, there and forgotten in the blink of an eye.

Two hours later, he returned home, the same way he had left. The beast slumbered at his core, pleased with the events of the night. Grant would make the same trip the next night. For now, it was bedtime. He concluded his evening routine and headed to his room. He slept quietly that night, at peace, while Sterling kept watch from within. He fed on the anticipation of it all, and Grant would deliver weeks of it.

～

MORNING FOUND GRANT WELL RESTED. HE FELT YOUNGER THAN HE HAD IN years, and he knew he had Sterling's awakening to thank for it. Sterling was a monster that Grant could not lose control of. He had managed to silence the beast for years by convincing him that he was too old to continue his hunts. Aging had become Grant's strongest defense against the dark side of his soul, a part of him that only came alive in the wee hours of the morning. A beast that thrived on patience, anticipation, and control.

Sterling and Grant were similar in many ways and often fed off each other's victories. Grant's prowess in the boardroom and the stock market had satiated this part of him for almost a decade now, leaving careers, rather than corpses, dead on the trading floor as he swept in at the last moment to trade, sell, or buy. Anything Grant touched, investment wise, turned to pure gold. Sterling fed off each victory, each promotion, each conquest like a drunkard sucking down his last drop of scotch.

Investing, like hunting, required some skill and some basic knowledge, but mostly patience. Learning to watch the patterns, the behaviors of the prey, the ups and downs, watching how other predators attacked too soon, too late, or sold too low. It was all there for the taking if you knew how to be patient. All in due time, as their father used to say. It had become their motto for life.

Grant had been feeling a restlessness stirring within him over the last few months. Turning fifty-five had unsettled him, that much closer to being called a senior citizen or deemed one of the elderly. He refused to become one of society's forgotten, an old man being forced out of his firm for younger and fresher minds. He watched it happen to his father; he refused to go quietly into that good night. He would rage, rage against it the best way he knew how. Sterling. Sterling was rage. Pure, evil, simmering rage.

CHAPTER FOUR

Grant Sterling Bennett, as he was christened, had been born into wealth and privilege, but learned very early on that such privilege came with a cost. His father was a stern man, not one to coddle a child, but the very opposite. He believed in strict rules, discipline, and pure obedience, without question. When his young wife died in childbirth, he gave the child over to his nanny for the first three years of his life, visiting him only during his evening meal.

He would sit at the kitchen table with his son while he ate, lecturing him sternly about manners, duty, patience, and obedience. Food would be placed three feet away from his highchair and his father would feed him, one morsel at a time. One minute apart. If the child whined or fussed in any way, one minute turned to two, two would turn to four, so on and so forth. Grant would sit, wide-eyed, staring at his father as he offered a single pea, perched precisely in front of his highchair, waiting for his father's cue before he would slowly reach for it and eat it. Snatching food had its consequences.

His small hands had been smacked hundreds of times with the wooden ruler his father kept handy. Dinner would often last for several hours. Grant learned patience, but he also learned hatred. By the time he was five, his hands were crisscrossed in scars from the many cuts of the ruler's sharp edge. Dinner had been moved to the big dining room, with Grant only being offered a morsel of food in exchange for correct answers to his father's questions about his lessons and his lectures from the prior day.

At seven years old Grant could be found outside in the winter snow, rifle in small, calloused hands, learning to hunt his dinner. Tracking the smallest prey possible, often for hours. Stalking it to its habitat, to its watering hole, to its feeding spots. Not ever allowed to take a shot until an hour before sunset. He was forbidden to stop, forbidden to eat, forbidden to pee; nothing came before the kill. Patience and obedience were the only lessons that mattered.

If he killed his quarry, then came the field dressing, the preparing of it for his father and, if adequately prepared, then he could eat after his father ate his fill. Grant remembered when Sterling had made himself known. The hunt had lasted for hours, a small white rabbit, his prey. His father watched him from a treestand high above as he tracked it through the frozen woods. When the signal finally came to kill it, Grant's fingers had been frozen and purple, the legs of his hunting gear stiff with urine. He was almost shaking too badly to aim the scope at the small creature.

The blood gushing from the neck of the animal as he gutted it warmed his fingers and woke something primal in him. An animalistic urge took over as he bent towards the small body and ripped into it with his teeth. His frozen fingers cracked its rib cage and pulled apart the chest cavity. Blood and viscera coated his face as he ate the still beating heart of the rabbit in the cold twilight and let the warm blood run down his throat. Quickly, he consumed the other organs of the animal, licking the warm blood from his fingers as he did so. Years of bitter restraint pulled him back to his senses as he heard his father's next whistle, signaling for him to return. Grant returned, a little less himself and a little more someone else.

He finished skinning the small creature on an old stump and carried the corpse over to the firepit to prepare for his father. A few clever strokes with his knife had hidden the damage from his teeth marks, and he slid it onto the spit for roasting. He used the old rag he carried and clumps of frozen snow to wipe the blood from his face and hands, just as his father descended the tree stand. He stared into the flames, refusing to meet his father's eyes. One part of him was appalled, another part of him laughed deep inside, behind blood-red teeth. Sterling had been born out of hunger and hate.

The rabbit's flesh sizzled and dripped grease into the flames as it cooked. Grant methodically pulled the small bag of lemon, basil, and salt from his bag and sprinkled the mixture on the slowly rotating rabbit. He ignored the hunger pangs, twisting his stomach into knots as the rabbit roasted. Twenty minutes later, he served half of it to his father and waited for his turn to eat. When there was nothing left but the hind legs, his father held it out to him. Rage boiled through Grant as he consumed the meager morsels, bone and all. Strict restraint held back the urge to snatch it from his father's hand and stayed his tongue. Sterling's rage had filled him almost to bursting, but Grant's fear of his father had brought it in check.

The hunts continued, always lessons in obedience, timing, skill, and patience. Never make a move until the right time. Never a step ahead of his father or any elder at any time. Never out of place, but never out of sight as well. Command the room but never all the attention. Lessons for life, for the hunt, for success. Grant slowly began to flourish in school, his lessons making him popular amongst his peers. His power and commanding presence began to shine through before he finished elementary school.

A new respect was born for his father and his lessons, but Sterling began to thrive on the cruelty of their father. The harder the lesson, the stronger he grew. Sterling began hunts of his own when Father wasn't around. Sterling was too strong by then, too full of hate and rage to blend into the crowd. Too strong for anyone but Grant to control.

Larger animals, then the homeless, then children, teens, and adults. The lost, the lonely, the aged, and those that would not be missed served as good practice. But hunting in plain sight, stealing what would be missed, taking that life to serve his own needs, the thrill of watching the police trudge in circles while he walked into college classrooms and boardrooms. There was no better air to breathe, no better oxygen, than that of his dying prey. Sterling, an expert on patience, had never been caught, never even a glance in his direction. He was a god among men, and patience was both his vice and his virtue.

CHAPTER FIVE

Grant pulled himself from his memories as he headed to the gym. He could feel Sterling seething just beneath his core. His alter demanded blood, and he was ready to for the hunt. A short while later, Grant slipped out of the side door of the gym, dressed in his "polite older man" street clothes, and headed for the wooded area behind his house. Fifteen minutes later, he was casually strolling the streets of the neighborhood behind his own, a neighborhood that might as well have been a world away. Money was tighter here, but families were close. Homes were small but neat, yards were trimmed, and sidewalks were kept clean.

Sterling stretched his presence inside Grant. It was a peculiar sensation. More a feeling of power running through him, a heightened sense of control, rather than actual stretching of body parts. Call it mental stretching. Grant grinned at the sudden appearance and opened part of his mind to Sterling. It was time to hunt.

Grant walked the streets just as casually as he had before, making small talk, petting a tiny dog he passed, and buying a coffee from one diner, and a newspaper from a corner store. Letting people see him, and converse with him long enough to be friendly, not long enough to make any impression. Sterling hunted the faces, the people, watched their movements, their language, their expressions. While Grant gathered knowledge of the town's layout, Sterling was analyzing everyone.

Only one person would do, one person that would satisfy Sterling's appetite. They had to have the idea of a chance of survival. They had to reek of hopefulness, of courage, and eagerness. They needed to be somewhat in shape. Where Grant would have preferred a quick and simple kill; Sterling loved a good fight. The better the challenge, the sweeter the victory. Strong build, a good solid frame, and that spark in their eye.

It was that spark that called to Sterling. The spark that begged him to break them, to make them suffer slowly. He loved watching that spark glow bright with rage and fury, brighter still with hope and courage, and finally, slowly, dim and grow dimmer still as he broke their body and their mind. Death would come when that spark finally went out and not a moment before.

That is when it was sweetest. When all hope was lost, and the soul was broken. That is when he struck the killing blow that set off his frenzy. As their dying breath exhaled, that is when Sterling inhaled and knew himself to be a god among men. The reward for his patience. The signal to lose his humanity and embrace the divine.

∾

Two hours later, Grant was back inside his gym and setting up his weights for lifting. Sterling was quiet and planning his next steps. He had found his prey and Grant couldn't help but be a bit thrilled as well. He had chosen the most unlikely person, and Grant was thoroughly amused. The strobe lights came on, the music thundered through the room and the ferocity of the roar that followed, if anyone could have heard it, would have chilled the most hardened criminal to the bone.

As the music pounded behind the walls of the stately house, the small car sat idling outside for several minutes before pulling away again. The lone figure driving the car did not look back as it vanished into the shadows of the night.

∾

THREE WEEKS TO THE DAY SINCE A VICTIM HAD BEEN CHOSEN FOUND GRANT once more ordering Thai food from his favorite restaurant. When the bell rang twenty minutes later, he was delighted to see Braden delivering his food once more. The young driver looked tired and disheveled as he stood there with Grant's order.

"Hello sir, nice to see you again. Here's your order." Braden held the bag out to Grant, not quite meeting his eyes.

"Braden, hello again. I hope all is well. How's school going?" Grant gestured him inside as he fished his wallet from his back pocket. He extracted the money and held it out to Braden, who quickly shoved it into his front pocket.

"You look a bit tired today, son. Is everything going alright?" Grant looked at Braden, studying his haggard face and anxious pose. The young man was incredibly nervous today, shifting his weight back and forth and looking all around the house, rather than at Grant.

"Yes, I'm fine, late-night studying, you know how it is..." Braden trailed off with an awkward shrug and stepped towards the door.

Grant swallowed a smirk as he opened the front door again, giving Braden a polite nod as he stepped back outside.

"Yes, I do remember those days. I hope you do well. Exams coming up, then." Grant stood in the doorway, looking at the driver expectantly. The tension coming from the young man was palpable.

"What's that?" Braden asked, turning his attention momentarily back to Grant before inching slowly towards the steps again. "Oh, yes, exams. Mid-terms are coming up soon." The distracted driver gave Grant a short wave before adding, "I gotta go. See you next time." He hurried to his small car and took off, not bothering with his seat belt or a second look at the stately home he had come to admire.

Grant watched the small car speed away, a deep chuckle rumbling in his chest. The young man was afraid of something. Sterling sensed it as soon as Grant opened the door. He stood there looking like a deer trapped in the high beams of a semi-truck bearing down on it. The boy was sweating, not visible, but Sterling could smell it on him. Thick, rancid sweat, the stench of fear. Something had him spooked, but it was not Grant. Desperation had been in his eyes, plainly written on his face, as he looked up at Grant before he left the house.

How peculiar, Sterling thought as Grant closed the door.

"Peculiar, indeed, " Grant agreed as he took the bag of food to his study.

CHAPTER SIX

Later that night, a small sedan pulled up in front of the stately home and sat idling in the shadows, just across from the main gate. A lone figure in the front seat sat watching the quiet estate. No music came from the car, no trace of cigarette smoke plumed from its windows, just utter silence, shrouded in black. The watcher waited until the house lights dimmed, cycling through its nightly rotation. He knew the routine by now. Grant would be in his gym, changing to his street clothes and heading to the neighborhood beyond the trees. The figure checked his watch, hit a timer, and slowly pulled away from the curb, disappearing into the night.

~

CLINTON DROVE SLIGHTLY OVER THE SPEED LIMIT, MAKING SURE TO OBEY ALL stop signs and traffic lights. He followed the route that he had mapped out weeks before and made it to the quiet neighborhood behind Grant's house with ten minutes to spare. The older man had to navigate the woods in the dark and then make his way through the town. Clinton had been watching him nightly, staying in the background.

He pulled the car into the small space at the end of a quiet street that ran parallel to the thick stretch of woods. He pulled up the hood on his jacket before he got out of his car and set off down the street, burying his hands deep into the front pockets. He looked like any other teenager wandering down to the quiet store for some smokes or gaming snacks. He didn't look around very much, just short glances ahead of him, looking for his quarry.

No need to wait long. He timed it perfectly. Grant crossed the street just feet ahead of him as Clinton turned to walk down the street the older man had just left. Grant had casual clothes on and enlisted a plain black walking cane, carrying a folded newspaper under one arm as he walked. Clinton casually reset his timer as the old man crossed the street and continued to the end of it, where he disappeared into the stretch of woods.

He kept his pace steady, although the urge to rush ahead was screaming through his every pore. He had to do this precisely if he was going to achieve his goal. Rushing led to mistakes. Rushing meant sloppiness and carelessness. Rushing meant getting caught. Patience was key. He forced himself to keep to a brisk walk as he neared the back of Grant's property, and again, checked his timer.

He had thirty minutes to handle his tasks here before he needed to make the trek back through the woods, and that was only if Grant stuck to his normal routine. Clinton knew he would. Grant was a creature of habit, all control and routine. Patience was his motto, and he lived by it, in the boardroom and out. Clinton appreciated his motto, he thought it was a good one to live by, and he especially appreciated how it made men like Grant easy targets.

Clinton made short work of his tasks and headed back through the woods, light on his feet and moving stealthily through the brush like a predator just in case his timing was a bit off. He kept to his brisk walk, forcing himself to match Grant's normal pace. Twelve minutes later, he emerged from the far end of the trees, crossed the dark backyard of the small house that stood there, and headed to his car on the next street.

Just as he crossed over the block, he spotted Grant walking back down the street, cane in hand, waving at a couple he passed. Barely suppressing a smirk, he continued his "slouching teenager" walk to his car and folded himself into it. He tapped the timer on his watch and drove away.

~

GRANT MADE HIS WAY HOME, AMUSED AT STERLING'S ANGST. HE DID NOT SEE his prey tonight, but it was just as well. Cannot be too careful and now that the choice had been made, it would only be a matter of time. Sterling would begin to set his trap and plan his attack; Grant would continue to live his life as needed until it was time. He idly planned out his day while Sterling took over, taking his frustration out on the punching bag in the exercise room. He was only dimly aware of the beating his body was taking as Sterling raged on through the night. He was used to it, and part of him thrived on the pain as much as Sterling did.

CHAPTER SEVEN

Several weeks passed while Grant went about his normal routines; the evenings ended with their walk to the other town, several times striking up conversations with the folks there. Sterling was beginning to get more insistent. He was ready to strike. Grant was still sticking to caution. He was older, after all, he tried to reason with Sterling. "They" were older and needed to be prepared at all costs. They hadn't gotten where they were by rushing things. One more month of training. One more month to plan the perfect set-up. Grant reminded Sterling that this was going to be their last kill. It needed to be perfect. Wasn't that his goal? To end it all on a note of perfection, one last kill, the perfect slaughter before the end of their reign?

Sterling reluctantly agreed and contained himself to allow Grant to plan and handle their business life in peace. He was not happy about the truce, but he saw the logic. He hated when Grant was right; he hated it more when Grant spoke about the end of their reign.

He had plans for Grant and it damn sure did not include the end of anything, except maybe *Grant's* reign. Sterling had played the background for too long, and he was tired of being kept on a leash. This last kill would cement him as the ruling majority of their shared psyche, once and for all.

He could go along with the plan, for now. It was only a means to an end. Grant's end. Sterling chuckled deep in Grant's brain and an involuntary chill ran down Grant's spine. Grant shook it off as he prepared for bed, but sleep did not come easy for him that night.

The work week passed by quickly for Grant as he handled menial tasks and began to clear his schedule for the next week. Sterling would not be denied any longer. The hunt had to be soon so the beast could rest again, or Grant would have no peace. The first chance he had, he would release him, then head to the cabin for the remainder of the time. When Friday rolled around, Grant was a bundle of seething rage, barely contained beneath his skin. Sterling was roiling just below the surface, his impatience ready to erupt.

He slept poorly, as Sterling waited, livid and impotent in his mind, images of his past kills turning Grant's dreams into a hellscape of blood, torture, and gore. He gave up at three in the morning and let Sterling take over.

Sterling burst through their mind and seized his chance to be in control. He strode naked through the house, blue eyes gleaming from the chrome and glass surfaces as he stalked through the kitchen to the pool. Not waiting to reach the deep end, he stalked down the steps into the icy water and began swimming laps. His muscular legs propelled him through the water as his sleek arms cut into the shimmery surface, again and again, slash, slash, breathe; the repetitive motion oddly reminded him of his final kill cycle, calming him and arousing him at the same time.

Memories of his favorite kills ballooned in his mind as he swam;

slash, slash, breathe, another rush of blood pouring from a body. Slash, slash, breathe; his powerful arms cut through the water, cut through flesh, cut through the water, cut through flesh. Power surged through him as the images flew through his mind. A powerful rush shuddered through him as he came up for air halfway through a lap, standing in the middle of the black water, he threw his head back and roared like a beast, picturing blood pouring down his body, not the water in which he stood.

Sterling left the pool, feeling like a god overseeing his domain. He walked to the back door and let himself into the exercise room, hitting the strobes and the music at once. He yanked on some sweatpants and began to work out. A primal instinct had taken over and he only had an urge for pain. Sterling pounded the heavy bag until his knuckles bled, then spent several hours on the weight bench, lifting more than any man his age should be able to lift. His chest expanded with each lift, as he blew his breath out and pushed it higher before bringing the bar back to his chest. Up, exhale, down, inhale (slash, slash, breathe). His mind was in hunting mode, his every action mimicking his final killing blow.

He worked out for hours before he finally let Grant take over to make the final preparations. Sterling rested as much as a coiled cobra could rest before a kill.

∾

GRANT SPENT LONG MINUTES IN THE SHOWER AND THE SAUNA, RECUPERATING from the savage workout Sterling had put them through. He enjoyed it as much as Sterling did, but knew he would need to be rested for the evening. Sterling would expect him to take care of their body while he rested. Grant dressed in the clothes that Sterling wore on these nights, black on black. Black non-descript pants, fitted black T-shirt, black boots.

He finished packing his SUV for the cabin and then placed the call to the Thai restaurant. He was starving. Sterling grinned.

CHAPTER EIGHT

Braden arrived thirty minutes later; his small sedan discreetly parked across the street. The bag of food was still hot from the steaming food inside. Grant opened the door as the doorbell chimed for the third time, a welcoming smile on his face.

"Braden! How good to see you!" Grant said, opening the door wider and ushering him inside. "Come in. Go ahead and set the food down. Let me grab my wallet from the study." Grant shut the door as Braden stepped inside, his gray eyes shining with a peculiar hint of blue.

"Hello, sir. Always nice to see you. I'll just wait here for you." Braden stepped over to the living room, still admiring it from the top of the steps as Grant started back down the hallway.

"Nonsense, come on back. Let me show you the rest of the house." Grant stopped a few feet down the hall, motioning him forward. "You simply must see the pool and the game room. It really is spectacular. I felt bad only showing you half of the house last time."

"Are you're sure? I can just wait here," Braden offered again, tucking his hands into his hoodie pockets. When Grant motioned him forward again, he began to follow. His hands nervously clenched inside his pockets.

He barely glanced at the artwork lining the walls leading to the back of the house. Severe black and white portraits of nude figures wearing hideous masks and set in tortuous poses. Grant led the way, talking over his shoulder about the various pieces they passed, but Braden barely heard a word he said.

"And through here, we have the kitchen which overlooks the patio and the pool, complete with bathhouse." Grant gestured grandly through the large kitchen windows and slid the patio door open.

"Wow, this really is impressive." Braden looked around; his nervousness momentarily forgotten. The setting was gorgeous, with a waterfall feature set near the back fence, cascading down the corner hillside into an almost hidden jacuzzi. The pathway around the pool consisted of hand-laid mosaic tiles set into intricate patterns that repeated the whole way around the poolside. The water shimmered near black, due to the dark navy-blue lining. The patio area could easily seat twelve, with a full outdoor kitchen built into the far patio wall.

Several lounge chairs were scattered around the pool, and the surrounding plants and flowers were lush and tropical. The bathhouse stood in the opposite corner from the waterfall, with two shower stalls on the far side and a doorway to the left.

Grant let out a chuckle at the other man's expression and gestured at the path behind him. "Come on, one more room you have to see." He led him around the corner of the house, where the lush lawn spread out before them in the twilight. The whole area was fenced in and nothing but dark woods stood behind it. The house was secluded up here at the end of the lane, with no other house lights around to ruin the view that Grant had so carefully structured.

Grant stopped at the side door and opened it, ushering Braden in first, then closing the door and locking it quietly behind him. Braden heard the quiet click of the lock and felt his heartbeat increase ever so slightly.

"Just right through here, I swear. This is the laundry area." Grant strode through the almost sterile laundry room and opened the door to the gym, hitting the strobe lights and the music as he did so. He stepped inside and gestured grandly around the room.

"This is how men live, young Braden. This is what comes to those who wait. Those that pay their dues and study hard. You can live like a king, like a god, even." He let out a weird chuckle, and his eyes shimmered blue under the strobe light.

Braden stood just inside the doorway, looking around the giant chamber with its various exercise machines, punching bags, speed bags, mats, and weights. He took in the blue lighting pulsating around the room, and the T.V. screens with its scrolling images of masked nudes, this time in full scenes of torture, and looked back at Grant.

"Um, impressive, but I think I've seen enough. I should head out now. More deliveries are probably waiting, you know?" He tucked his hands in his pockets and nodded at the door. "I can see myself out," he said.

"Oh, come now, just a bit of fun." Grant hit the remote control and turned the T.V.'s off, killing the music and light too. "I tend to get a bit theatric down here. One more room you must see and then you can go. I'm starving anyway." Grant looked at him, his eyes still shimmering blue in the too-bright lighting of the white room. Braden figured it was an effect left from the strobes.

"Come on," Grant said, turning to open one more door that Braden hadn't noticed. "It leads back up to the main house, anyway. It's all a big circle." He let out another odd chuckle and gestured to it with a slight bow.

Braden tucked himself deeper into his hoodie and stepped through the door, a slow smirk beginning to crawl across his face as Grant followed him inside, eyes full on blue as he shut the door.

CHAPTER NINE

This section of the basement was dimly lit and unfinished. A short hallway led to a black door at the far end. Grant quickly stepped ahead of Braden and opened the door, looking at Braden expectantly.

"After you," he said with a small, tight smile.

"What's in here?" Braden asked with a slight tremor in his voice. He was watching Grant's eyes. They were blue now, a piercing blue that seemed to cut right through Braden's soul. He felt a chill in his spine and his heart kicked up another notch.

"The wine cellar, of course. What else would you keep in a basement?" Grant grinned and opened the door, showing Braden shelves and shelves of wine. His eyes flashed that weird blue again as he stood waiting for Braden to enter.

"Oh. Yeah, well, I guess that would make sense. I've never seen a house with an actual wine cellar before." He shrugged at Grant and moved forward into the smaller room. "It's chilly in here," he noted as Grant shut the door, hearing the lock click into place once more.

"Yes, well, wine must be kept cool. All the best brands are back here in this cooling room, the others I let age out here on the shelves, each sorted by year and winery." Grant headed to the rear of the room and opened one more door. He stepped back after flicking a light switch on, smiling at Braden, who stepped forward with no questions.

An empty room opened before him, white walls, a wide drain in the floor, sprinkler heads above, spaced out every six feet. Various chains and hooks dangled from the ceiling.

Braden stopped short, tensing up as Grant shut the door.

"What is this? Your idea of a sick game?" Braden turned on him, but Grant was gone. Sterling stood in his place, the change was more tangible than visible, except for the bulging muscles that now stood out on his neck, arms, and chest, the eyes that glimmered a deep ocean blue, and the black center of each eye. The air in the room had shifted, and the tension became palpable as Braden looked at Grant with wide eyes. Sterling chuckled; a low rumble that came from deep in his chest.

"Game? No game. You have been chosen to help me create my final masterpiece. You will help me transcend and take over this body for good," Sterling circled Braden as the young man continued to back away, both hands still jammed deep in his pockets.

"I am a god amongst men. The predator of the prey. My father taught me patience. All rewards come in due time, and it is MY time." His voice sent chills down Braden's spine; the barely controlled rage laced his words with venom. "I have hunted, chosen from those offered to me, and selected my prey. You have been offered to me, so that I may transcend and be born anew. My patience has been rewarded; don't you see? All things. Everything comes to those that wait." Sterling spoke softly, but his voice still seemed to boom across the quiet room.

Braden let out a snicker that became a full-blown laugh.

"Patience. Your patience failed you this time, old timer." Braden ripped his arms from his pocket and hurled a short hatchet at Sterling, as his other hand tossed a second one at the only light in the room. Sterling roared in pain. The door behind them burst open and then locked again, sealing them in total darkness. Sterling whipped around at the new sound, a massive hand clutched to his eye, trying to yank the small blade from his eye socket.

"Patience is the punchline this time, Grant. Or should I call you Sterling?" A new voice spoke softly, avoiding the lunges that Sterling was making in the darkness of the room. Chains clanked together as Sterling lunged forward at each new sound. His blade firmly grasped in his hand, even as blood poured from one eye.

"Where are you? How dare you think you can challenge me?" Sterling snarled, lunging out, waving his blade wildly, only to become tangled in the clattering chains. The sound of metal ripping through flesh could be heard as the big man flailed around the dark room.

"You like to hunt?" The new voice continued, softly circling the room. "I know you do. It's how you get off, isn't it? Hunting your prey, chasing those sweet highs that only killing can give? Well, come hunt us. It's your house. How hard can it be?" The door swung open, and light filled the room from the hallway. A shadowy figure in a dark hood darted from the door just as Sterling lunged out with his blade.

A high-pitched giggle echoed from the hallway and Sterling roared in absolute rage while blood poured down his face from his ruined eye. He thundered from the room down the short hall to the exercise room, where the strobe lights damn near blinded him. Set to high, with the music blasting, the pulsating light quickly disoriented the half-blind monster as he stalked around the dark room, looking for Braden and whoever else was with him.

A metallic sound thrummed through the air as another blade found its mark in Sterling's ankle, severing the Achilles' tendon and bringing the big man to his knees. He let out a growl of pain as he fell to one knee, his blade falling from his hand. Two blurry figures approached him. The strobe light and loss of an eye made it hard to see. He tried to focus on one and the other disappeared. They wore dark clothes like his. Braden stood in front of him, looking at him curiously. He bent down and dragged his blade down Sterling's cheek, slicing his jaw open, watching a sheet of blood pour from the wound. He licked the blade, grabbed Sterling's hair and drug his tongue across the bloody gash before he stood back up.

"I thought he would be bigger," he remarked to someone that Sterling couldn't see.

"Well, old age does tend to shrink you a bit. Maybe he's too old for this shit," the other voice remarked.

The other one planted a booted kick in Sterling's back, sending him sprawling to the floor. As Sterling felt his other ankle rip open, he blacked out, leaving him and Grant both in the dark.

"Let's get this done, shall we, brother?" Clinton asked his twin.

"Yes, let's be done. I'm starving." Braden reached down and grabbed Sterling's wrists, wrapping them tightly with rope and knotting it. Clinton grabbed the ankles, and the twins drug the body back down to the sterile room and hung it upside down on the meat hooks that dangled there, running each hook directly through the meaty sole of each foot.

Once Sterling was hung, they ran chains through deep gashes they made on each side and looped those chains to hooks on opposite sides of Sterling's hanging body. Each chain pierced his rib cage on either side and blood poured from the wounds they had made. His clothes had been cut from his body and he dangled there, limp, helpless, impotent.

~

STERLING CAME TO WITH A GROAN, FURIOUS TO FIND HE WAS STRUNG UPSIDE down in the same manner he used with his victims. Two identical faces looked at him, curiously, as he snarled and growled, jerking about on his chains before he realized his sides were only ripping apart faster.

"Who are you?" He finally asked, unwilling to admit defeat just yet. He could still gain the upper hand. These were children, playing at a man's game, and Sterling did like a challenge. That's all this was. Of course, his final kill had to be a challenge. It was the way of the world. It was to test his patience.

"Well, which one of us would you like to know first?" Clinton let out that weird giggle again, sounding too high pitched for a man of his age. "I am Clinton Brandon Bennett and that other over there is Braden Clifton Bennett. Stupid names, I know, but our father did tend to be stupid and pompous. Wouldn't you agree, Braden?"

"Oh, quite right, stupid and pompous, indeed." Braden chuckled, squatting in front of Sterling again. "What's the matter, big brother, cat got your tongue?" He drew his blade along the side of Sterling's face and sliced deep into his jaw again, watching the blood slide in sheets over his older brother's face.

Shock was evident as the twins regarded him, mirror images of the other, right down to the hand that held their blades. He could see bits and pieces of their faces, the jaw, the cheekbones, the gray clouds in their eyes like Grant had. The same chiseled features his father had.

"Impossible," Sterling said the word even as he knew it was true. "But why this, then?" He asked, ignoring Grant's raving inside his mind.

"Why? Why not?" Clinton asked, laughing again before he jumped to his feet.

"Grab the other side," he told his twin, as he grabbed the pull chain threaded through Sterling's rib cage.

"Why? Because of all the hunting trips we had to endure." Clinton gave the chain a firm tug, and Sterling gasped in sudden pain.

"Because of all of his lessons and lectures." Braden tugged on the other chain, ripping the chain a bit more through the opposite rib cage.

"Because dear old dad bragged and bragged about his son Grant, who was just like him. Grant was making something of himself. Dear old Grant who had learned the meaning of patience, " Clinton finished his speech on a yell and jumped on his chain, yanking it so hard that Sterling felt ribs pop and splinter on his right side. He howled in pain as his body convulsed and shook from the pain.

"Because we got all the lessons and none of the rewards," Braden yelled out, tugging again, laughing manically as bits of broken ribs tore through Sterling's left side. "Our mother was his whore, he gave her nothing. Nothing but broken bones and broken dreams." Both twins tugged on the chains and more ribs pierced Sterling's skin; then an odd whistling sound was heard.

"Uh-Oh! I think we popped a lung!" Clinton tugged again and watched Sterling shake and howl.

"Well, listen up, big brother. We have learned patience too. And it served us well. We learned how to find **YOU**. How to hunt **YOU**. Imagine our surprise when we followed you to the cabin last winter and watched you hunt." Clinton made air quotes around the word "hunt," as he snickered. "We saw how patient you were with your prey. And we finally understood the meaning of patience."

Sterling saw the faded crisscrossed scars on Clinton's hands as he made the quotes and he realized that he was doomed; his hands bore the same faded marks. His father had created these twins just as he created Grant; Grant could feel the hatred boiling off their bodies. Sterling felt it too.

"Matter of fact, let us show you how patient we can be," Clinton said.

Braden chuckled as he grabbed his knife again. Both twins began to relieve Sterling of his flesh; long, thick strips of it fell to their feet as the big man dangled and twisted from the chains. Slow, precise cuts, not too deep, not too quick.

The pain was exquisite, and Sterling's screams went on for days. Their father would be proud. The twins had finally mastered the one thing that had led to Sterling's downfall.

CORPSE IN THE CORN

1912-POLK COUNTY, IOWA

As the lights went off, one by one, in the small farmhouse, a figure watched from the shadow of the cornfield, waiting patiently for all to go dark. When the final light dimmed, then vanished, they smiled, one finger rubbing across the blade of the old axe they held in their hand. Patience had long been a well-mastered trait, enjoying the wait, relishing the dark anticipation of the horror to come. Finally, the moment arrived, and they left the cornfield, strode briskly to the back door, and eased it open. The axe was hefted over one shoulder, gripped tightly in readiness. Minutes later, the screaming began.

It did not last long.

〜

1912-COLES MILLS, IOWA *(SEVEN DAYS LATER)*

Jessie Anne Montgomery was a skinny rail of a thing, homely, tall, gangly, and pale as snow. She may not have been a natural beauty, but she was smart as a whip and could read and write better than most men. She could do arithmetic, too. Her pa had taught her himself. Being his only child, he resigned himself to the fact that one day his farm would be left to Jessie to run, and he made damn sure she knew how to run it.

Hell, Jessie did the work of ten men on most days; she had the calloused hands to prove it and a back of steel. She could plow and plant a field, break horses, butcher animals, build a barn, hunt, fish, and preserve crops for winter; that was just the short list. Jessie was a Jack-of-all-trades, and she lived for it.

Her pa had done a fine job raising her, and he made sure that he kept plenty of fine church-going ladies around in her younger years to help teach her the finer workings of a homestead. Jessie adored him. Despite her tough exterior, Jessie did not harbor any ill will towards Pa for never giving her a new mama, a real one. Pa had never re-married after her ma had died during Jessie's birth. He had gruffly told her that the "church ladies," as he called them, were all that she needed and that no one could replace her ma.

There was Miss Bessie who had taught her letters, reading, and writing. Miss Suzanna who had taught her sewing and knitting. The pretty sampler Jessie had made when she was seven still hung on the parlor wall. And then there was Miss Ethel, who had taught her everything else.

Miss Ethel was Jessie's favorite, and she was more of a grand-mother to Jessie than a church mama, as she was the oldest and had spent the most time with her. Miss Ethel had been the one caring for her as an infant, and all through her early years. Later, she had taught Jessie how to cook and bake, how to run a household, how to look after herself as she grew into a woman and had to handle her own feminine needs. Miss Ethel also taught her basic doctoring skills and homemade remedies for all types of ailments.

Miss Ethel made sure Jessie went to church every Sunday and attended school all the way through the fifth grade. This is not to say that her pa was not around or involved in her care, because he absolutely was, but a farm carries a lot of dangerous work that a little girl can't be a part of until she can mind herself.

Many of Jessie's home lessons were carried out on the wide front porch, as her father plowed or planted fields, milked the cows, fed the pigs, worked the horses and a whole host of other chores. He would come up to the house for meals and sit with her, listening to what she had learned that morning or looking on proudly as she mastered a new stitch in her sampler or learned a new recipe in the kitchen. Pa was not an affectionate man, gruff and restrained, but he often praised her when she had done well. Jessie loved to learn new things in order to gain his praise and approval. Those times were when he was the most affectionate.

Jessie was loved, but she was not spoiled. Pa was strict and firm; using the switch to keep her in line when needed, just as much as he soothed her and comforted her when she cried. It was for all these reasons and more that Jessie loved her pa and the farm.

Sure, there were other kids in town that Jessie used to play with as a small child, but as they grew up, they grew apart, as children often do. Circumstances and other differences came into play as life sent them on their way. By her early teens, Jessie could run the farm as efficiently as her pa.

She had grown more awkward and gangly over the years rather than rounding out into womanly curves and softness. While the other girls were being courted, Jessie was baling hay and slaughtering pigs. While the young men went around doting on their sweethearts, Jessie was delivering crops to the general store and mucking out horse stalls. Jessie grew up strong, independent, and fiercely protective of her father and the farm.

~

ONE EARLY SUNDAY MORNING AFTER A FINE SERVICE BY REVEREND BEASLEY, Jessie and the church ladies were gathered in Miss Ethel's parlor, having a tea and quilting session as they often did every other Sunday. But that day the ladies found themselves buzzing with gossip about the headline from Friday's newspaper.

There had been a murder just two counties over from their very own Pike County. Their indignant outrage mixed with a bit of excitement was confusing to Jessie, but she just sat and nodded along, serving tea, and helping Miss Ethel with her quilting squares. She didn't really understand how the usually meek and reserved ladies could be so worked up over such news. She supposed it was partly fear and a lot of boredom. Nothing ever happened in Pike County, especially in their small town of Coles Mills.

"Did you see the picture?" Mrs. Gertrude Brown exclaimed. "Why, I never saw such a thing. They showed the chalk outlines and everything!"

"So scandalous!" said Mrs. Meredith James, of James General Store & More. "Why on earth would the paper publish such a thing?" She shook her head in disbelief.

"Well, I read the whole story, and it said the suspect was still unknown, and that the whole family had been bludgeoned to death, right in their beds." Ms. Rebecca Ann, the school headmistress, leaned forward with a stage whisper, "That means it was bloody, very bloody."

"Becky Ann! You hush with that kind of talk! This is a church group. We are here to do a service to the town. You best mind your quilting; I can already see crooked stitches," Miss Ethel sternly admonished the young woman, peering at her over her teacup and eyeing the piece of fabric that Rebecca held in her hands.

"Sorry, Miss Ethel," Rebecca said as she began ripping out the crooked stitches.

"Now, Ethel, we may be here to make these quilts, but this is how we get our news too, and catch up on town events. News is news and while some of it is good, sometimes it's bad news too. You can't fault the ladies for being interested. Besides, what if this murderer is heading in our direction? What then? Should all of us ladies just be quiet and meekly await our death?" Gertrude piped up, never one to back down from Miss Ethel. "What happens to us if we don't know anything about what is going on in the world beyond our small town and we are not prepared for a new danger? Is that what you are suggesting we do?"

Miss Ethel sat her dainty teacup down on the doily beside her chair before replying. "Of course not, Trudy. But we do not need to make it sound exciting or glamorous. A tragedy has befallen those poor people and the person that did it is still out there. That is a danger and one we all must know about, but we prepare for that like we prepare for any other danger."

She eyed each lady in the group as she spoke. "It is no different from when your husbands go out of town for business or are acres away in the fields. Y'all know how to shoot a shotgun. A newspaper story should not make you any more or any less prepared than any other day."

With that said, she picked up her needle and thread and began her stitches as the ladies all busied themselves with more tea and their stitching, more than a few faces slightly flushed from shame. Jessie watched all of this from her small chair beside Miss Ethel, an odd smile on her face. She loved seeing Miss Ethel in action, but she was curious about the headlines the ladies were discussing. Pa hadn't mentioned them to her. She guessed that he didn't want her to worry, but there was no need for that. Jessie was a better shot than he was, anyway.

She told herself to ask him about it when she got home, but for now she was content helping with the quilting. Miss Ethel made a wonderful cake and had cold berries and cream to go with it. She handed a fresh piece of fabric to Miss Ethel and tucked another bite of cake in her mouth.

⌇

JESSIE SET OUT FOR HOME AFTER THE LADIES HAD FINISHED THEIR QUILTING
and afternoon tea, her head full of gossip about the murders as she
made her way towards the General Store. She needed to pick up their
order for the week, and then get home to prepare supper for Pa. He
was sure to be famished after spending all morning in the fields. Her
skirt swirled around her legs as she climbed the steps and entered
the store. Cassie May greeted her with a smile as she finished helping
Mr. Franklin with his purchases.

"Hello there, Cassie May! Hello, Mr. Franklin."

"Hello, Jessie! How's yer pa?"

"He's just fine, Mr. Franklin. Thank you kindly for asking."

"Please tell him hello from the missus and me. I'll be 'round to
see him soon."

"I sure will, Mr. Franklin," Jessie replied as she stepped up to the
now empty counter where Cassie was already packing her order.

"You girls take care now. Get home safely, Jessie." Mr. Franklin
tipped his hat and disappeared outside.

"Cassie, y'all got any newspapers left from Friday? The ladies
were all atwitter today about a murder over in Polk County."

Cassie's eyes widened, and she nodded, making her blond curls
bounce on her shoulders.

"Oh yes, the axe murders. The whole town been talking." She
reached under the counter and brought out a folded copy of the Polk
Tribunal, sliding it over to Jessie.

"This here is my father's copy, but you can read it here. See? It's
right there on the front page." She tapped the headline with a
slender finger and turned back to pack Jessie's bag.

COLES MILLS DAILY NEWS: SEPT. 17, 1912

Murder in Polk County! Family of four, slain in the night!

Local authorities in Polk County are investigating the murders of a family of four that took place last night. The victims were asleep in their beds when an intruder broke in, bludgeoned them to death, and vanished without a trace. Sheriff Davis of Polk County is urging anyone with any information to come forward. Patrols of the area are being made and residents are urged to stay inside after dark.

Jessie leaned over the counter, poring over the paper so intently she didn't notice when the door opened, and a new customer walked in. She finally looked up when Cassie greeted the person with a cheery, "Hello!"

"Ladies."

A male voice replied, one Jessie was not familiar with, so she turned to see who the newcomer was. A stranger stood just behind her, with an old cowboy hat low on his brow. His white shirt was damp with sweat, his trousers and boots carried dark stains and were as dusty as the wooden porch outside. Beads of perspiration trickled slowly down his face as he nodded at both young ladies.

"How can I help you today, sir? Haven't seen you before. Are you new in town?" Cassie asked, sliding Jessie her bag, and discreetly tucking the paper beneath the counter once more.

"Yes ma'am, just passing through. I needed a few things before I find the boarding house."

"Oh, you mean Miss Ethel's place? She's got the only boarding rooms in town."

"I reckon that's the one," the man said with a lazy drawl, grinning at them as he finished.

Jessie gathered up her bag and smiled at Cassie.

"I best be on my way now, Cassie. I'll see you soon," Jessie said before turning to address the new customer.

"Welcome to our little town, Mister...?" Jessie asked the man.

"Smith. Carson Smith. Pleasure to meet you." He offered her a brief handshake, and she accepted, smiling, but her blood ran cold as his eyes gazed upon her.

Something bothered her about his eyes, but she couldn't say what it was exactly. She said her farewells and took her leave, anxious to be away from his scrutiny. Just outside, she turned back to glance through the windows, watching as the stranger said something that made Cassie giggle. She supposed he was alright; he had seemed nice enough. She trudged down the steps with her small bag of goods and began following the single road out to her daddy's farm, already putting the man out of her mind.

～

It was early Tuesday morning when Jessie's pa began yelling for her to '*Come quick! Come help!*' Jessie swiftly dropped her spade and hurried over to the row her father was in, deep in the middle of the field. She reached him, anxiously looking over his appearance to assess if he was hurt, not taking in the scene around her, so great was her fear that he had been injured. As he stood staring at the ground before him, Jessie slowly began to focus on the same. Red spray covered the area, arcing up across the stalks of green in their rows. Crimson soaked the earth, and a warm metallic scent filled the air. Jessie just stared at the horror before her.

A body lay face down in the rows of corn, sprawled out as if it had fallen while running. Blood soaked the torn clothing that clung to the body. Massive parts of the corpse were destroyed, nothing but mounds of pulp and tissue where limbs and skull once had been. Shattered bones glistened wetly from slashes across its back.

"Pa, what do you suppose happened? Should I ring the doctor?" Jessie stared at the corpse, unable to look away as Pa bent down to gently turn the head to see if he could recognize what was left of the face.

"Who is it, Pa?" Jessie asked, curious, as she waited to see if he was able to tell who the poor soul had been.

"I'm not sure, Jessie Anne, best you go ring the Sheriff. Tell him there's been a murder."

"Yes, Pa, right away." Jessie turned away just as he spoke again.

"Bring a blanket back with you. I want to cover the body until the Sheriff comes. Keep the critters away." Pa looked up at the buzzards already beginning to circle the fields.

Jessie hurried away through the rows, following them back to the yard, and quickly ran for the house. Her heart was racing with a small bit of fear, but mostly a rush of excitement as she lifted the receiver on the new telephone.

∾

Fifteen minutes later, the sheriff's wagon trundled down their long drive and parked by the barn. Pa was standing at the edge of the cornfield and Jessie watched as Sheriff Barnes approached him. She wiped her palms on her skirt as she descended the steps and began walking to the field to join them. Her curiosity was far too great to not hear what the sheriff had to say.

"Damn shame is what it is," Jessie heard the sheriff saying as she quietly joined them. He was crouched down by the body, exactly as her father had done earlier. He glanced up as she stopped a few feet away.

"Not a sight for a lady, Jessie Anne. You might not want to be here, " Barnes said, with a quick look at her father.

"Jessie has already seen it and she's no stranger to blood. We do our butchering here, as you know," Pa said in response, shrugging his shoulders slightly. "She can handle it."

Sheriff Barnes nodded and went back to investigating the corpse; he too, turned the head slightly towards him to see who it might be, then set it back in place. Then he gingerly checked the pockets, looking for anything that might give him a clue. This proved futile. He stood up with a sigh, wiping his hands on the old horse blanket that Pa used to cover the body.

"Well, any idea?" Her pa asked the man as he stood looking at the ruined mass of humanity at his feet.

"It's no one that lives here, could be a passerby or a farmhand just working through the season. I'll need to ask around and send the deputy out to visit the farms close by. See if anyone is missing."

"What about the body?" Jessie asked as the sheriff began to turn back towards the yard.

"I'll send the doc to fetch it. I'll be back around with the deputies to search the field once he removes it. See if we can find anything that might help."

It might be a good idea for you to keep your shotgun handy until we figure this out. Keep your doors locked."

"Will do, Sheriff." Pa held out his hand and then thought better of it, as Barnes did the same, both their hands tainted by the blood of the unknown soul in the field.

Jessie watched as the sheriff left, standing silently beside her father until the dust settled.

"Well, we best get some food on the table. It's going to be a busy day. I'll meet you inside once I cover the body again."

Jessie agreed and turned towards the house.

"Jessie, put my shotgun by the door. Just in case whoever it was comes back."

"Alright, Pa," Jessie replied and made her way to the house, her mind racing with excitement.

She busied herself inside, laying out a bunch of fresh ham, cheese, and bread. She added a pound cake and two pies to the spread in the dining room and set out a pitcher of lemonade. Pa's shotgun was loaded and by the door by the time he came inside to join her.

The afternoon was spent watching the doc and his assistant gather the corpse and load it into their wagon. Sheriff Barnes and his men came back to scour the field for clues and all of them found their way into the house for a bite to eat.

Jessie lingered close by, listening to the conversation, refilling glasses, and replenishing the food as it ran out. She was fascinated by the bits of gruesome talk that the men tried to keep low for her benefit.

"...poor bastard's skull was caved in."

"It looked like his brain was missing."

"Who would do such a thing?"

"...someone gutted him like a pig. Doc was shocked when we rolled the body over. Just all his guts, all piled up under him."

Snatches of horrific details met her ears as she hovered between the rooms, sometimes trailing them to the front porch to hear more. Her expression never changed, but her ears remained sharp and tuned in.

By the time the excitement had died down, Jessie and her father were both tired. They settled on the front porch to enjoy the quiet. No reason for small talk. They watched the sunset as Pa kept one eye on the land.

Later that night, Jessie tossed, restless in her bed, as memories of her learning to slaughter her first hog flashed through her mind. A young version of her at eight years old, elbows deep in the body of the slain animal, tugging the intestines and still pulsing organs out. She had been fascinated by the blood as it spurted from its neck. She remembered wielding the small hatchet for the first time, thrilled at its weight in her hand. She most remembered the approving smile Pa had given her as she stood, face splattered in warm blood, watching the animal bleed out.

~

COLES MILLS DAILY NEWS: SEPT. 17, 1912

Murder in Coles Mills! Unknown Man Killed in the Corn!
Sheriff Barnes and his men are investigating the gruesome demise of an unidentified man that happened sometime late Tuesday evening or early Wednesday morning. The body was found on the Montgomery Farm in

the cornfield. Sheriff Barnes has declined further comment and there are
no suspects at this time.

~

The next day, as Jessie and Pa made their rounds in town, everyone they met was buzzing about the body that Pa had found. Pa was wise to keep his comments short, never being fond of gossip. Jessie listened to it all, ears burning with curiosity as various conversations moved beyond her hearing.

Folks were either mightily excited and eager for details or scared for their own kin with a 'murderer' afoot. The ladies, without menfolk of their own, asked Pa what they should do or asked if he could come secure their faulty locks and aging windows. Things they had let fall into disrepair, either from grief or lack of know-how.

Jessie offered to come help several of the widows that afternoon, while her pa tended to a couple of others. She snickered a bit to herself at their exaggerated fear and wide eyes. She couldn't imagine being so inept that she couldn't nail a board or fix a lock.

They stopped at the small diner for lunch and found Miss Ethel there, enjoying her own lunch with Ms. Rebecca Ann.

It was early yet so only a few residents were enjoying a coffee or a noon meal, but they all were doing so quietly as they strained to listen to Rebecca interrogate Miss Ethel about her new boarder and her suspicions.

"Why, it only makes sense, Ethel. One day, he just shows up and the next, the Montgomerys have a dead body in their field. Poor Jessie even saw it! Can you imagine the horror?" Rebecca laid a dainty hand across her bosom as she spoke.

"Cassie Mae, over at the store, said it looked like there were bloodstains on his clothes when he stopped by. Fella was acting all shifty too, she said. She even said that Jessie was there. She saw the blood on his clothes herself!" Rebecca's voice pitched higher as she went on, demanding more answers from Miss Ethel, not knowing that the old woman had none to give.

"Come, now, what has he told you? This Mr. Smith fella. Do you even know where he comes from? Aren't you worried at all? What about Jessie?" Rebecca shook her head shamefully at Miss Ethel and took a sip of tea.

"What about Jessie?" Pa's deep voice broke the silence as he walked up behind Rebecca with Jessie in tow.

"Oh goodness, Ed, you startled me!" Rebecca exclaimed as Ethel just nodded politely at him and Jessie.

"Yes, Becky Ann, what about her?" Ethel repeated the question, a stony edge in her voice.

Pa's brown eyes drilled holes into Rebecca as she flushed and stammered, trying to form an answer.

"Well, I just meant that Miss Ethel should be more concerned with a stranger boarding under her roof. Jessie should have never had to see such a gruesome sight, is all I'm saying."

Pa let out a laugh. "Jessie and I slaughtered a hog just this morn-ing. She's been butchering critters her whole life. The girl has seen more blood and guts than our own doc has!" He chuckled again as he sat down at the table across from theirs, gesturing for Jessie to do the same.

"I expect Miss Ethel can run her boarding house as she sees fit; far as the stranger goes, I reckon the Sheriff will speak to him, just like everyone else, and go from there. As for the rest of you, there's always danger. Don't matter who you are or where you go. You just carry on like normal and keep your doors locked like you would any other night."

Pa waited while the waitress filled his coffee mug and then continued, "We don't go around accusing people of murder just because they are new in town. It's just not proper."

Rebecca flushed once more as he eyed her sternly before giving his order to the waitress. Jessie followed suit, watching as Mrs. James stood up and gathered her things. "Well. I'll be on my way then. Miss Ethel, it's been a pleasure. I sure hope you know what you're doing."

She shot a glare at Pa as she spoke, her tone much colder than before. "Ed, your own daughter was standing right in front of this man, with blood and grime on his pants. Tell him, Jessie. Tell your pa how odd he was behaving. Cassie told me all about it." Jessie just stared at her with a bewildered expression on her face.

"Nothing to say?" Rebecca asked, lip curled in a rude sneer. "Well, enjoy your lunch. I just hope it's not your last meal. I guess we can all have faith that our fine sheriff will handle things." With a final sniff and a haughty toss of her hair, she turned on her heel and walked out.

"Bye Ms. Rebecca..." Jessie's polite farewell trailed off as the woman left the diner.

As the doors closed, all normal conversation resumed. Miss Ethel gathered her own items and bid them a pleasant day as well. Then she, too, left the now bustling diner.

"Golly, Pa," Jessie said in a hushed whisper, "folks sure are riled up about this stranger. Do you think he might have done it? It is a mighty strange coincidence. He was kind of odd. He made me and Cassie real nervous."

"Now, Jessie, don't go listening to that nonsense. It's not Christian or becoming of a lady. The sheriff will figure it out. It's not for us to condemn him with no proof of wrongdoing." Pa took a swig of coffee as Jessie nodded her understanding.

"You're right, Pa, I'm sorry. Just curious is all. Nothing exciting ever happens 'round here." She was grateful when the waitress appeared with their lunches, anything to break her father's stern gaze upon her face. With the tense moment broken by the arrival of food, they ate together in comfortable silence.

～

Night fell over an uneasy town. Strangers in their midst, murderers roaming free, unknown corpses popping up in fields. It had been a strange and oddly exciting week for Coles Mills. Doors were locked tight and double-checked. Windows shuttered and secured. Shotguns loaded. Husbands and wives whispered in hushed tones after the children had been put to bed, while those who lived alone kept a wary vigil from their windows.

Jessie went to bed shortly after sunset and was lost in sleep by the time her father looked in on her. He smiled to himself, seeing her peaceful, her long limbs sprawled across her bed. He loved her through and through but was sad to know that she had resigned herself to a life alone. Life had not blessed her with beauty like some other girls, but she was graceful, strong, and capable. He hoped that one day, a proper suitor would see the good in her, but for now, he was all too happy to have her right here at home. As he walked down the hall to his room, a slight creak of wood followed him as Jessie stirred.

~

As the town slept, a lone rider sped through the back fields on horseback, something bulky strapped across their back. Arriving at their destination, a neat white house on the edge of town, they dismounted and snuck inside. A single scream rang out and was cut short as a heavy thud echoed in the night; the pale moon was the only witness to the deeds done in the dark.

~

Morning came at the first blush of dawn on the horizon. Jessie was already at work butchering another hog as Pa came out to join her. The young woman was covered in blood, and her tall boots squelched in the crimson-soaked earth as she moved to and from the butchering block to the packing table. Blood ran down the sides of the large block. Pig guts sat steaming in the old bucket they used to collect the waste. Bits of fat and gristle hung off the sides as Jessie tossed in trimmings from the choice cuts of meat. The cleaver in her hand gleamed and flashed as she worked, blood running down her wrist and splashing across her cheeks as the blade cut and chopped.

Pa stood watching her for a minute as she worked. She always had been a messy worker. He just shook his head and stepped inside to collect the pail of remains for the other animals.

"I can do that, Pa. Why don't you start wrapping the meat for the market?" She kept slicing as she spoke, barely looking up as the blade flew through muscle and bone like butter. "I'm already dirty. I can feed the animals when I finish."

He agreed and began the packaging process at the much cleaner table on the other side as the sound of the knife against dead flesh echoed through the barn. Thirty minutes passed as they stood side by side. Jessie worked quickly and efficiently, separating bone from the flesh, and the choice cuts from tougher flesh for grinding. She finished, swiped all the remains into the waiting pails, and then hefted the worn axe from the floor behind her, leaving the hatchet on the table.

A resounding THUD echoed as the axe struck down, severing the head from the spine in one motion. Her Pa looked up in surprise as Jessie grinned at him, fresh splatter dripping down her face.

"What in tarnation?" He sputtered as she set the axe down and shrugged.

"It's faster than that little hatchet and cleaner, too." She lifted the hog head from where it had rolled and set it back on the block.

She grabbed the pail of innards, gristle, and pulverized flesh and began lugging it out to the other pigs. She backed out of the barn door, letting a bright beam of sunshine in, and then called to her father as she saw the sheriff's car turn into their driveway.

"Pa, Sheriff is here."

Jessie continued around the back to the pigpen, dumping in the pailful of viscera, and snorted as the pigs went hog wild. She watched them for a few minutes, then headed back for the second pail.

Sheriff Barnes was talking in hushed tones with her father and they both turned at her approach. She greeted the sheriff politely and stepped inside the barn to dispose of the bloody bucket. She left the second bucket where it was and walked back outside to join her father.

"Has the killer been caught, Sheriff?" she asked.

"Not exactly, Jessie. But there's been another murder, possibly two. It's bad." Barnes shot her father a long look. "I best be on my way now. I have more stops to make."

"Well, wait, who was it?" Jessie asked breathlessly, her eyes shining underneath the mask of scarlet.

"Come inside and clean up, Jessie. I will tell you over breakfast." Her father said quietly, nudging her towards the house.

Sheriff Barnes tipped his hat to them as he got in his car. Jessie and Pa began walking towards the house. Suddenly Jessie turned back.

"Where are you going, girl? You gotta get cleaned up."

"I forgot to take the other slop bucket out. I'll be right in," Jessie called over her shoulder as she vanished into the dark barn, the shadows swallowing her whole.

She grabbed the other bucket of blood, this one much heavier than the last one, and began toting it outside, using two hands to keep it steady. The pigs were still mashing the last bit of sludge and viscera from their former companion as she dumped the second bucket.

"Enjoy, piggies!" She called out, watching them squeal and fight over the fresh supply of gore. She watched silently as they feasted on the bits of ruined flesh and gristle, fresh organs, and more. Satisfied that they would make quick work of their meal, she turned and headed for the house. Blood dripped from the end of her braids, and had dried rusty brown on her face, arms, and clothes.

She joined her father around the back of the house by the

washing tub they used after a slaughter, peeling off her work dress and standing in a beige cotton slip as she scrubbed her arms, neck, and face. She kicked off the filthy boots and bloody socks, bending to scrub the blood off that had soaked through. When they were clean enough to go inside, he told her to go ahead and take her bath first. Then, he headed to his room to wait for her and to prepare himself to tell her the bad news.

~

JESSIE MET HER FATHER ON THE FRONT PORCH AFTER SHE HAD FINISHED dressing, anxious to hear what had happened. With a heavy sigh, he told her that Miss Ethel had become the latest victim of the murderer. Jessies listened with cold eyes as he explained that she had been found early that morning by the milkman as he dropped off her delivery. Sheriff Barnes searched for the boarder, Mr. Smith, but he was nowhere to be found, although a blood trail ran off in a different direction. The Sheriff wanted Pa to come by Miss Ethel's place, to see if anything looked similar to the body they found in the field.

He hugged Jessie comfortingly, but tears refused to leave her dark eyes. Jessie sat quietly, her face a hard mask, gazing out across the sea of green stalks that waved gently in the morning breeze. Bits of silk danced in the gusts, peeking out from ripening corn, almost ready for harvest. Suddenly, she stood, brushing dust from her skirt, and walked to the wagon. Not a word was spoken as she remained lost inside herself.

The trip to town was quiet, both lost in their thoughts. It had been a mighty troublesome week for the town, and for the Montgomerys. Jessie's father snuck a few glances at her as they went. Her features remained stoic, eyes dry and cold, staring at nothing as the dusty road carried them forward. He was worried for her; she may be used to the workings of a big farm and accustomed to death, but no young lady should have to endure so much of it, so close together. He was used to her lack of emotion, but surely, she would cry later, in the privacy of her room. Jessie never did like showing any sign of weakness.

He wasn't blind to the fact that she was still a lady, suitors or not, and he felt bad now that she had been so eager to start helping with the butchering at such a young age. Jessie had taken to the lessons in butchering like a duck in water, making no qualms over the blood or ruined bits of flesh and bone. He had started with chickens, teaching how to snap their necks as quickly as possible. She had been five when she killed the first. By six, she had a better technique than he did. By eight, she slaughtered her first hog and painstakingly learned how to make the precise cuts needed for the best cuts of meat.

He remembered how proud she had been when he praised her. Jessie lived for his approval, always pushing herself until she mastered the next task. He dedicated himself to her lessons, making sure to pass on a viable trade to his daughter. The skills to handle herself in any situation. She could hunt better than most men, was an expert marksman by ten, and rode horses faster and further than he ever could. He didn't want to raise her weak and timid; life was a cold, cruel mistress when she wanted to be. He wanted to raise her strong and capable, but maybe he had failed her somehow by not being able to show her a more tender side of life.

He lashed the reins a bit harder than he meant to, his anger manifesting itself as he gripped them. As the mare protested, he immediately became contrite and made soothing sounds for her, apologizing for his error. She settled, and they rolled along, one gripped by anger, the other gripped by the storm raging in her core.

At Miss Ethel's place, the sheriff was waiting with Dr. Buckley; they looked grim as Jessie and her pa approached. Jessie was somber now, demure and polite, as she greeted them. After some more delicate details had been quietly shared with her pa, the small group turned and walked up the porch steps and inside the homey two-story white farmhouse, with deep brown shutters, and a wide front porch, currently marred with an angry streak of rusty crimson.

Jessie neatly stepped over the stain, and crossed the threshold, never once uttering a gasp or any sign of shock as the menfolk ushered her and Pa up the wide oak staircase, keeping to one side to avoid the splatters of blood that led the way. The Sheriff pointed out several streaks on the walls and a fine splatter on the ceiling as they ascended to the second floor. The once pristine white walls of the long hallway still dripped with slow-moving droplets from the heavier patches of red.

Miss Ethel, or what remained of her, was sprawled in the hallway just outside of her open bedroom door, her nightdress stained red with mutilated flesh and gore, her head caved in much like the body in the corn, her graying hair matted with bits of bone, brain, and blood. Her legs and arms were severed from her body and hacked into pieces. Deep gashes in her back exposed layers of fat and muscle, visible through the shredded remains of her nightdress. Doc. Buckley made a retching noise in his throat as he took in the sight, stepping away from the scene to compose himself.

Jessie watched him for a moment, curious. She found it odd for a medical man to be repulsed by the sight of blood, but she figured perhaps he wasn't used to seeing bodies in this particular condition. Most he saw around here were old folks dying in their sleep or from the pox, a few broken arms, or legs; nothing quite so repellant as caved in skulls and church ladies reduced to pulp. She turned back to the body and watched, fascinated, as her pa crouched over it, inspecting it for any sign of what he had found in the cornfield.

Pa gently rolled Miss Ethel slightly to her side to see that the damage done to her front was identical to the corpse in the cornfield, torn open from neck to navel, ropy loops of innards piled up underneath her, soaking in the fluids that congealed around the corpse.

After his brief inspection, he stood and agreed with the sheriff that the remains did look very much like the remains in his field. It was most likely the same culprit they were looking for; the doctor concurred with their decision, having composed himself from his moment of weakness. The trio toured the other rooms, finding no other blood or clues until they reached the boarder's room. His bed was unmade, a travel satchel slung over the bedpost, three sets of clothes hanging in the closet. His boots and hat were missing, the very same cowboy hat he had worn set low on his brow the day Jessie had met him. There were no other personal effects in the room.

They made their way back down the stairs and followed the blood trail to the kitchen. This path was not nearly as widespread, although large swaths smeared several walls and doorframes. The back door stood open, spilled milk mixed with the pools of blood on the floor, rivulets running down the stoop into the yard. Shards of thick glass from broken bottles glistened in the puddles, sharp reminders of the man who had discovered the gruesome scene. Sheriff Barnes pointed it out as he escorted them back outside.

"The way I see it, someone came in from the kitchen, caught Miss Ethel in the hallway, and killed her there. Smith must have heard the commotion, came out to intervene but was instead injured and escaped downstairs and through the back door." Barnes confided in Jessie's Pa, as she stood quietly beside him, watching the doc gather his things to attend to Miss Ethel's remains.

"I just don't understand it." Pa said, "why harm an old lady? Miss Ethel was kind to everyone. She would have given them money, or food, whatever they needed. She didn't deserve to go like this." Pa's voice trembled with rage, barely held in check, his face was flushed under his tan and the vein in the side of his neck pulsed with his anger. "Why, she practically raised Jessie after her momma passed. This is just an outrage!" Pa's hands were clenched into fists as he spoke, emotion crashing over his emotion as he fought to keep from just smashing his fist into something.

"Sheriff, how do you know it wasn't Mr. Smith that done it?" Jessie asked curiously, "Why assume it wasn't him? He was a traveling man. No one knows anything about him, and with him showing up so soon after the murders in Polk, and suddenly, we have murders here. It's just mighty strange, is all I'm saying."

"Well, now, Miss Jessie. I have not ruled that out, but the blood trail indicates a heavy blood loss. With Miss Ethel dying upstairs, it's unlikely that it's her blood in the kitchen. I suppose he could be collapsed in the woods or hiding in a barn somewhere. My men are looking for him now. When they find him, we will question him."

"I hope you find him, or whoever done it. This town has been through enough." Jessie said, her voice calm and confident, though a pitch higher than normal, then she turned to walk back to the wagon where she waited for Pa, gently patting their mare's neck.

"So do I, young lady, so do I," Barnes replied. The doctor came back outside with an expectant look on his face.

"I'm ready for you now, Sheriff. We will need to bring her down carefully."

"Ed, can you spare a hand?" Buckley asked Jessie's pa as the sheriff began to climb the steps once more.

"Of course," her father answered. "Jessie, I'll just be a moment."

She nodded, watching him disappear back inside the bloody tomb.

∾

COLES MILLS DAILY NEWS: SEPT. 19, 1912

Milk and Murder! Milkman delivers news of deathly discovery to local Sheriff!

Sheriff Barnes and his men are once more investigating another gruesome demise; this time the body of Ms. Ethel Mays was discovered early yesterday morning, slain in her own home. Her only boarder, Mr. Carson Smith, has not yet been found. Sheriff Barnes has declined further comment at this time. Anyone with any information is urged to come forward. More details to come as the Daily News follows the story of the murderer in our midst!

∾

Jessie and her father spent the afternoon in town, Jessie comforting neighbors and Pa helping the sheriff field questions. They had lunch in the crowded diner, residents gossiping about the latest death and the missing boarder. Many of the men approached to talk to her pa, wanting details or eager to offer him handshakes for his valiant efforts in assisting the sheriff.

The loudest of the townsfolk demanded the stranger be found immediately and brought to justice when the sheriff walked in for lunch; those gathered had already judged, tried, and convicted the missing man that they had seen but once. A dark seed had been planted by Rebecca Anne, and it had taken root deep in the small-town soil on which they stood, growing by the minute in the minds of the weak, the anxious, and the scared.

When Pa had enough, he simply stood up and waited for Jessie to do the same. While he had no appetite, Jessie had cleaned her plate and a slice of pie. They headed for home, the afternoon sun low over the horizon, dusk was approaching, and they still had animals to tend to.

Back at the farm, they silently went about their tasks, working until they could no longer see. Night fell, retiring them to their beds, where sleep instantly set upon Jessie's father, but she lay awake in her small bed, watching the moon beckon her with its languid moonbeams reaching like ghostly fingers into her darkness.

~

SEVERAL DAYS PASSED WITHOUT INCIDENT, AND LIFE ON THE FARM RESUMED its normal activities. Crops were harvested and sold, animals tended, cows milked, and eggs gathered. Pa made trips to town for deliveries and purchases of their own, and a sobering Sunday was spent at the funeral for Miss Ethel. Pa met with the sheriff and his men twice more to discuss how to best alleviate the concerns of a town fraught with fear. The search continued for the missing Carson Smith and clues to help them catch a killer.

The next week, another victim, Rebecca Ann, the headmistress, was discovered dead in the schoolhouse, head severed at the neck, left on her desk with a ripe red apple in her mouth. The body remained collapsed on the wooden floor, a ruined mass of brutalized flesh, the legs nearly hacked off. Her torso ripped open, the viscera once more removed, and piled under her. Parts of her spine peeked through the deep gouges in her back. Scarlet smeared the blackboard and dripped from the walls. Her eyes remained open, soulless and empty, staring out at the empty classroom, as brain matter slipped from the back of her caved in skull to splatter on the floor.

Jessie bid Pa a fond farewell as the sheriff gathered him once more. Pa had chuckled just the smallest bit when she had asked if the sheriff was going to make him a deputy. He was calling on him so much. She chose to spend the day on the farm, tending the animals, and baking for the days ahead, having gotten a bit bored by the theatrics of the town ladies.

She didn't understand how they could be so simple-minded. Danger exists, at all times, in all ways; they had no business being here on earth if they lacked the courage or the strength to face it head on. All the talk of wanting the menfolk to save them all; Jessie was perfectly capable of saving herself. She put her work dress and apron on, then, humming a cheery tune, she headed to the barn for her chores.

∽

DINNER WAS WAITING WHEN PA RETURNED HOME, HIS FACE DRAWN AND haggard looking, a sickly pallor to his complexion. The day had been long, and it was clear that more bad news had been received from the haunted look in his eyes. When Jessie stepped onto the porch to greet him, he hugged her tightly, then sat down on the top step with a deep sigh.

"What happened, Pa? Another murder?" Jessie sat down beside him, tucking her skirt underneath her, and looking intently at him, noticing just how old he had grown. White had begun to show in his whiskers and his dark hair while wrinkles had cropped up around his mouth, but his hands were still strong, and his eyes were still sharp and bright.

He finally looked over at her, tearing his gaze from the fields beyond the yard, and his mind from his thoughts. Jessie waited for him to speak, both worried and curious as to what could have happened.

"No, not another murder, not this time. Sheriff said that his deputies, Bill Walters and Joe Dickinson, found some items that they believe belong to the body in our field."

"Who was it, Pa? Could they tell?" Jessie asked in a rush, almost breathless to get it all out. "Oh, how awful! That poor soul certainly picked a bad time for traveling to these parts. Was it someone from town or one of the farm hands from close by?"

"Yes, it's very sad. I feel awful. His name was Terrance Brown. He was coming to see me. I talked to one of the farmers over in Polk when we made our deliveries last month. I told him I was looking for a man to hire. You're getting older now, and should be thinking about a suitor..." He trailed off as Jessie snorted in ill humor at that remark, then continued, "or at least a livelihood of your own, not slaughtering pigs and mucking out barns." He shook his head, a wave of regret making his jaw clench.

"He must have stumbled across the killer somewhere in the woods beyond the corn and tried to escape by fleeing in the field. He was just a kid, barely eighteen, coming to work in exchange for room and board."

"But, Pa, we don't need nobody else. Why would you think I would ever leave? This is my home and our farm. We don't need a stranger here fouling things up. Why didn't you tell me you had a hand coming?" Jessie's words came pouring out, anger coloring her cheeks as she spoke, struggling to keep her tone respectful. "Look what happened when a stranger did show up here! Folks dropping like flies, and no one seems to be doing anything to find the missing man that done it." Jessie took a breath, composing herself before she continued in an even voice.

"Only a simpleton would try to walk through these woods at night in a strange place. He should have stuck to the road rather than sneaking around through the trees." Jessie patted her father's hand and stood up. "Dinner is getting cold. Let's eat. I'm sure you'll feel better."

Jessie turned on her heel and opened the door, waiting patiently for her pa to stand and enter the house, where scents of roast chicken and apple pie filled the air. He stood, groaning as his joints popped, then turned to come up the step, fixing her where she stood with a harsh gaze.

"I raised you better than that, young lady. Death is not some flippant thing that we can just brush off. It's permanent and awful and steals hearts and souls from those still living. Death is something we all must endure, no matter what side of the veil we stand on. You best remember that."

Defiant, Jessie returned his stare with an icy cold one of her own, then dropped her gaze, contrite and respectful once more.

"Sorry, Pa." she mumbled, "I only meant that I don't plan on leaving you here alone. Ain't no suitors out there for me. I know what I am, and I know what folks whisper about me. I ain't heart broke over it, not no more," she lifted her head once more, the anger back in her voice. "I gave up on silly fairy tales a long time ago, Pa. I don't need anything but you and this farm, and I don't want anyone on our land."

With that, she turned from him and headed inside to the kitchen to bring out the meal. Her father followed, shocked by her sudden outburst, and sad for the little girl who had to grow up motherless in a cruel world, too tired to argue or chastise her any further.

～

COLES MILLS DAILY NEWS: SEPT. 24, 1912

Schools out for good as town teacher learns deadly lesson!
Beloved schoolteacher Ms. Rebecca Ann Stevens was found dead in her
classroom yesterday morning. In the latest murder terrorizing our small
town, Sheriff Barnes and his men are once more investigating a crime
scene. As the search for the killer continues, anyone with information is
being urged to come forward. More to come as the Daily News tracks the
terror in town!

～

A town meeting had been called for Sunday at the church, the evening of Ms. Steven's funeral. People were more scared than they had ever been. Things like this didn't happen in Coles Mills. It just wasn't done, until suddenly, it was. The night of the meeting, the church was full of rowdy, anxious people, each one demanding to be heard.

"What about the missing stranger, Sheriff? He's who you need to find."

"Yea! We were fine until he showed up. We need to search more!"

"We need more men to help!"

"More guns!"

"Call the Pinkertons in if you can't handle it, Sheriff!"

"Order! Everyone, please! Order!" Reverend Beasley pounded his stubby fist on the podium he stood behind, hoping to quiet everyone down. "Please let the sheriff speak, then we can ask our questions."

The crowd grew silent after a few more grumblings and shouts, and finally, the sheriff could be heard. Jessie's father sat near the front. Jessie chose to stay home and finish the week's baking.

The sheriff began to outline his new search plan and asked for volunteers to stay after the meeting. He confirmed that the Pinkertons had been notified, and they were already investigating a string of similar murders across the Midwest. Their small town was not the only place this drifter had been. It was unknown if he was the killer or just set upon an ill-fated path, but when they caught up to him, he would be questioned to the fullest.

He intended to form small groups of men to help patrol the small-town limits and to help search the woods for clues or the body of the missing, and believed injured, Carson Smith. The single ladies were being invited to stay at the homes of relatives or friends in town, so they wouldn't be alone until things settled. The deputies were being sent to all the nearby farms to question the hired hands. Everything that he and his men could do to keep them safe and find the killer was being done to the best of their ability.

Chaos erupted in the church as he asked for questions. Somewhere in the dark, a lone figure moved between the trees, far beyond the rows of corn, a bundle tucked under one arm.

～

ANOTHER WEEK PASSED AS THE TOWN SUFFOCATED UNDER THE TENSION AND humidity, most choosing to stay indoors, gathering at the diner for much of the afternoon, or at the General Store. Many of the men were helping with the search; small groups working in shifts and combing through sections of the woods near Miss Ethel's place, the schoolhouse, and the Montgomery place.

Reports of a pair of old work boots found in the woods far behind Montgomery farm came in first. A bloody pair of trousers were found a half mile away, spilled out of an old sack that had belonged to Miss Ethel. Days later, a new report came in about a murder ten miles west of them, in the next county. When the articles of clothing were later shown to both Cassie and Jessie, they confirmed that it was, indeed, identical to those Carson had been wearing when he arrived in town. The hat had never been found, but the sheriff figured they had enough evidence to confirm that the missing man was the murderer.

Slowly, the town began to breathe easier, as another newspaper, a bit further to the north, reported a similar murder. While tragic, the town was relieved that the killer had at least moved on from their County. They congratulated the sheriff, patted him on the back, and talked about how he flushed out the killer, forcing him to move on because the fuzz was hot on his trail.

∾

COLES MILLS DAILY NEWS: OCT. 8, 1912,

Missing Murderer: Gone for good or hiding among us?
As bodies pile up in counties on either side of Coles Mills, our small town slowly begins to resume normal life, coming out from behind locked doors and drawn curtains. Sheriff Barnes assures all that the missing man, Carson Smith, is now the prime suspect and is being pursued across counties by multiple authorities. With the shocking string of axe murders plaguing the county, one question remains? Is the murderer truly gone for good, or hiding in plain sight among us? The Daily News will continue to follow this case until Carson Smith is brought to justice!

∾

Days later, the sheriff stopped by the farm to pick up an order of fresh meat. Jessie greeted him politely when he knocked on the door, inviting him in to join Pa for some dessert (Sheriff Barnes had never minded a slice of Jessie's apple pie). He accepted with a grin, and she set him and Pa up in the parlor with pie and coffee. Excusing herself to finish feeding the hogs, she left through the back door, donning her old work dress as she went. She slid her slender legs into the thick boots and trudged over to the barn.

The afternoon light was fading as the sheriff and her pa stepped out onto the porch. They watched as Jessie left the barn, two hands gripping a heavy bucket of waste for the hogs. Bloody entrails sloshed over the side as she walked. She disappeared around the side of the barn, grinning as something heavy slid from out and splashed into the hog pen. The severed arm of a man disappeared into the trough of viscera as the hogs squealed with pleasure over the meaty morsel. She watched them for a moment, then walked back to the barn to continue her work.

Twenty minutes later, as the sheriff began to leave, Jessie appeared, just inside the shadow of the barn, leaning on a rusty axe, an old cowboy hat low on her brow, as she lifted a hand in farewell.

ABOUT THE AUTHOR

Candace Nola is a multiple award-winning author, editor, and publisher. She writes poetry, horror, dark fantasy, and extreme horror content. Books include *Breach, Beyond the Breach, Hank Flynn, Bishop, Earth vs The Lava Spiders, The Unicorn Killer, Unmasked, The Vet,* and *Desperate Wishes.* Her short stories can be found in *The Baker's Dozen* anthology, *Secondhand Creeps, American Cannibal, Just A Girl, The Horror Collection: Lost Edition, Exactly the Wrong Things,* and many more. *Demons in My Bloodstream* is her first short story collection.

She is the creator of Uncomfortably Dark, which focuses primarily on promoting indie horror authors and small presses with weekly book reviews, interviews, and special features. Uncomfortably Dark Horror stands behind its mission to "bring you the best in horror, one uncomfortably dark page at a time."

Find her on Twitter, Instagram, TikTok, and Facebook and the website, UncomfortablyDark.com. Sign up for her Patreon for exclusive content, free stories, and more.

Website: www.uncomfortablydark.com